1960

The

Trail

of the

Spanish

Horse

The

Trail

of the

Spanish
Horse

JAMES WILLARD SCHULTZ

Illustrated by Lorence Bjorklund

1 9 6 0

HOUGHTON MIFFLIN COMPANY BOSTON

𝕿𝖍𝖊 𝕽𝖎𝖛𝖊𝖗𝖘𝖎𝖉𝖊 𝕻𝖗𝖊𝖘𝖘 𝕮𝖆𝖒𝖇𝖗𝖎𝖉𝖌𝖊

Contents

Publisher's Note

No American author has written with such intimate knowledge and sense of adventure about life with the Indians as James Willard Schultz. He is the author of 37 books that are unequaled in their authenticity and the flavor they give of a vanished way of life.

In 1877 when he was 17 years old, Schultz took a trip up the Missouri River into a West that was still untamed, still the domain of the Indian. It was the beginning of a new life for him and one that suited him perfectly, for as he later wrote, "The love of wild life and adventure was born in me." After a season with a young trader named Joseph Kipp he decided to throw in his lot with the Indian. As Apikuni, or Far Off White Robe, he became a member of the Blackfoot Tribe, took part in their war parties, adopted their ways, and married an Indian girl.

But though he felt his real home was in the Lodges of the Blackfeet, he did not abandon white civilization. In later years he used his considerable influence to improve the treatment of the Indian by the U.S. Government.

Schultz's novels sprang directly from his own experiences and even the most exciting episodes are apt to contain more fact than fiction. We are proud to publish this new edition of *With the Indians in the Rockies, The Quest of the Fish-Dog Skin* and *The Trail of the Spanish Horse* with illustrations by Lorence Bjorklund. The passage of time has made the Schultz books classics, but it has in no way dimmed their freshness for another generation of readers.

The
Trail
of the
Spanish
Horse

CHAPTER I

IN WHICH SUN DOGS APPEAR

TOWARD the close of a warm spring day in April, 1867, luminous spots appeared both on the north and on the south of the setting sun. I noticed them as I returned to our lodge, after watering Is-spai-u and picketing him upon a patch of new sprouting buffalo grass close in front of camp.

"Sun dogs!" I said to myself. "Strange that they should appear at this time; they belong to the cold days of winter."

My heart misgave me. I had lived so long and so intimately with the Blackfeet that I had come largely to share their beliefs. Sun dogs are a warning of misfortune that would soon befall either the tribe or some member of it.

I went to the lodge and sat beside my almost-brother, Pitamakan — Running Eagle. We shared the warm robe couch on the right of the fireplace. Across from us upon her couch sat his sister. At the back of the lodge was their mother, White Wolf's head wife. The chief was visiting some-where in camp, and we awaited his coming to have our evening meal of boiled boss buffalo ribs.

We were a hunting party of only forty lodges of the Small Robes clan of the Pikuni, or South Black-feet. The rest of the clan, including White Wolf's other wives and children, were with the great camp of the tribe at War-Trail Fort, the trading post that my Uncle Wesley had built two summers be-fore at the mouth of the Musselshell River. We had come a day's journey up the river from the post and had not found game plentiful; on the morrow we were to go up Flat Willow Creek to the foot of the Snow Mountains, where we should probably find all kinds of game.

When I went inside Pitamakan was rubbing marrow grease into the stock of his rifle, a fine weapon that carried a ball weighing thirty-two to the pound; as he energetically polished the dark wood he sang the wolf song of good luck for the hunter. He sang it four times, the sacred number, and his mother and sister and I, as we listened to him, were uplifted by the noble rhythm of the song and the deep, clear voice of the singer. He ended with a "kyi!" of satisfaction and set his weapon against the back rest at his end of the couch. With happy smiles the women resumed work on the moccasin uppers they were embroidering.

We heard approaching steps, and White Wolf thrust aside the door curtain and came in. He let the curtain fall back into place behind him, slowly walked past the fire and with a heavy sigh dropped down upon his couch and exclaimed, "Sun has painted himself!"

"Kyai-yo!" mother and daughter cried in one breath.

"Trouble comes!" said Pitamakan, glancing at his rifle.

"I saw the paintings as I came into the lodge," I said.

"Pass out the food," said White Wolf to his wife. "Let us eat quickly, for I must get Red Eagle to pray for us all."

"You shall have sacred food along with the boiled ribs!" she exclaimed, and upon each dish of the meat she laid a small lump of pounded and dried cherries. From those we broke small pieces, buried them in the ground and cried, "O Sun! O Earth-Mother! We sacrifice this food to you! Pity us and let us survive all dangers that may be closing in upon our camp this night!"

That was a silent meal; each one of us was wondering what might be the danger of which the sun had given warning.

"Sun in his mercy gives us his sign that we are in danger, all of us or some of us, here or in the great camp down at the fort," said the chief when we had finished. "It is for us to pray and make

4

sacrifice to the gods and use every possible precaution against surprise by the enemy and against mishaps in the hunt. You, boys; you, woman mine and daughter — but, no; I go now to Red Eagle; when I return I will speak to you more fully about it."

None of us spoke after the chief had gone out. Mother and daughter washed the rude wooden dishes and the horn spoons and laid them away but neither of them resumed her quill embroidery. We all four sat humped over upon our couches, staring at the little fire of dry cottonwood branches; and of the four I was certainly the most down-hearted; I had broken my uncle's commands. How I wished that I were back once more at the fort, with Is-spai-u safely locked in the stable inside the stout, cannon-protected stockade!

Presently we heard old Red Eagle shouting invitations to some of the head men of the camp to come to the unwrapping of his sacred thunder-medicine pipe. I went out and looked at Is-spai-u hungrily nipping the new sprouting grass. I patted his sleek back and looked off down the moonlit valley and was minded to saddle him and go back to the fort as fast as he could carry me. But I was afraid of the night and of the hidden dangers of the trail.

"Is-spai-u," I whispered to him, "we will start for home at daybreak!"

As I turned back, a dozen voices in Red Eagle's lodge began singing the first of the songs of the thunder medicine — the Song of the Buffalo. I imagined the old man and his head woman bending over the sacred roll of the pipe upon the couch between them and with closed fists imitating the ponderous tread of the buffalo in time with the slow, weird, heart-thrilling tune. I even caught some of the words of the song: "O ancient ones! O you, our food, our raiment, our shelter! Let us survive! Do let us survive the dangers that encompass us!"

It was a song prayer to the first buffaloes — they that had the power to take the form of man and to speak man's tongue.

6

"Almost-brother," I said to Pitamakan as soon as I was again beside him on our couch, "we must stand guard over our horses this night!"

"Yes, we must do that," he agreed.

"Let us go now and protect them."

"It is too early to do that; war parties do not attack a camp until the fires have died out, and the people sleep. Let us remain here before this cheerful fire at least until my father returns."

"Very well," I answered. But how I wanted to take up a robe and my rifle and go right out to Is-spai-u! Fear of the amused laughs and gibes that would greet my going held me to my seat.

Over in Red Eagle's lodge the tune changed.

"The Antelope Song! Let us sing it with them," said the good mother. We did so. Then in time with them we sang in turn the Song of the Wolf and the Song of the Grizzly Bear.

In the other lodge the sacred roll was now outspread and the gorgeously feathered and furbanded stem of the thunder pipe was revealed. Now the old medicine man was taking coals from

7

the fire, laying upon them a pinch of dried sweet-grass and purifying his hands in the scented smoke.

"Ha! Now he lifts the sacred stem! And now he dances with it!" Pitamakan cried.

There came the wild burst of the Thunder Bird dance song, deep-toned and profoundly sad. It gripped our hearts, that song; it made us shiver. I saw mother and daughter bow their heads in prayer and lift their hands to the sky. Then the song was suddenly drowned by booming guns and frightful yells on all sides of our camp; and within the lodges women and children shrieked, and men called out to one another. A bullet tore into our lodge and seared the top of my right shoulder. Another spatted into the fire, scattering coals and ashes over the women.

"Lie down, you two! Lie flat!" Pitamakan shouted to them as we seized our rifles and ran out into the night, he to the place where he had picketed his and his father's favorite horses, I to my green-grass patch. Then cold sweat broke out upon me. I felt that I wanted to die: Is-spai-u was not there!

I was so dazed by my loss that I know not how long I stood there or what was going on round me. I finally realized that some one was calling "Otah-toyi! Otahtoyi!"

"Here!" I managed to answer, and then Pita-makan put his hand on my seared shoulder, and the fearful smart of it brought me to myself. The shooting and the yelling of the enemy had ceased. Somewhere out in the night they were speeding away with our best horses. After two years of wily endeavor they at last through my fault — my dis-regard of my uncle's commands — had Is-spai-u in their possession. I groaned aloud. I could never face my uncle again.

"Well, it is done," said Pitamakan. "We can do nothing until morning. Come!"

I followed him. We could hear women at the upper end of the camp wailing for the dead; we passed several groups of men talking excitedly.

As we entered our lodge, White Wolf came close

upon our heels. "Well, I suppose they have Is-spai-u?" he said.

I nodded.

"And the five of ours that I picketed," Pita-makan told him.

He gave a heavy sigh. "Who would have thought that we should be attacked so early in the night? How soon they came after Sun's warning to us! We had no more than begun to make sacrifices and pray! They killed Short Bow and Sun Weasel and wounded Big Bear's woman, Good Singer," he said.

At that mother and daughter covered their heads with their robes and wept.

Soon the head men of the camp began to come into the lodge by ones and twos and threes until there was room for no more; but all were silent until White Wolf had filled his big pipe and started it round the circle.

Then one of them said, "I wonder if they have driven off our herds as well as our fast runners?"

"I doubt it," the chief answered. "They have

Is-spai-u, you see, and will run no risk of our over-taking them. They are heading for home as fast as they can go."

The talk went on, but I soon lost the sense of it; I was too miserable to listen. I kept saying to my-self, "I have lost Is-spai-u! What, oh, what shall I do!"

Let me tell you about Is-spai-u, the Spanish horse. Some summers before One Horn, a great warrior of the Pikuni, led a war party south into the always-summer-land, as we called the Mexican country. A year later he appeared in Fort Benton, riding a fine black horse and suffering from an old wound. He was the sole survivor of his party, and he was so ill that my uncle and his wife — my almost-mother, Tsistsaki — had taken him into our quarters and nursed him as best they could. He took my uncle's hand and with his last breath said to him, "Far Thunder, from the time you and I first met we have been friends. You have been very good to me. And now we part; this night I am going upon the long trail to the Sand Hills.

I give you my black horse. I took him in battle with the Spaniards in the always-summer-land. North, south, east, and west he is the swiftest, the most tireless horse upon all the plains. I know that you will be good to him. There! I can talk no more!"

So the brave old warrior died, and with loving care the women wrapped him and his weapons in many a blanket and robe and gave him fitting burial below the fort.

Now, long after that event my uncle mounted Is-spai-u one day and ran a herd of buffalo that had come into the bottom. With bow and arrows he killed twenty-seven of them, the largest number by far that one hunter had ever killed in a single run, thanks to the wonderful speed and endurance of the horse. Some Kootenay Indians who were present and saw the chase offered their all for him, but my uncle only laughed at them. They returned to their own country and spread the fame of the wonderful runner among all the West-Side tribes. Later when some of our *voyageurs* arrived at Fort

Union they told about the wonderful black runner, and the fame of him spread from here to all the tribes of the plains, until our friends tried to buy him, and our enemies to steal him. Then in the early summer the American Fur Company went out of business, and my uncle decided to go into the trade for himself and build a fort at the mouth of the Musselshell on the greatest war trail in all the Northwest. There while we were building the post we were beset by war parties of Crows, Assiniboines, Yanktonnais, and others, who tried to take Is-spai-u from us, and in our fights with them we lost more than one of our *engagés*.

Now through my perverse disobedience Is-spai-u was in the hands of the enemy. Exactly four weeks before this day, when the ice on the Missouri broke up, my uncle had set out for far-away St. Louis in a keel boat manned by four *voyageurs*, in order to buy a large quantity of trade goods and bring them to our fort in the first steamboat of the season. On the evening before he went he had left my almost-mother, Tsistsaki, Solomon

Abbott, brave, faithful plainsman that he was, and me in full charge of the fort and all its activities. To me he had said, "You, Thomas, my boy, must take the best of care of Is-spai-u. You will feed him well and regularly, of course, and give him what exercise he needs. But mind this: spring has come; enemy war parties are abroad in the land; in no circumstances will you ride Is-spai-u out of sight of the fort!"

"As you say," I had told him, and I had kept my promise until White Wolf and some of the Small Robes clan decided to go up the Musselshell for a short hunt, and Pitamakan begged me to go with him. Tsistsaki and Abbott had readily agreed to let me go, and Abbott had said that he himself would take care of Is-spai-u while I was away; but then the thought had come to me to take the horse upon the hunt and have some wonderful buffalo runs with him. All that evening and all that restless, wakeful night I resisted the temptation, but with the coming of the sunny day my fears had vanished. Protected by forty lodges of warrior

14

hunters, Is-spai-u, I said to myself, could come to no possible harm. Early in the morning I took over to camp some bedding to be loaded on one of the pack-horses, and at the same time I told Pita-makan that he was not to wait for me; I would take the trail later on and overtake him and the outfit before midday. I had several good buffalo runners of my own in White Wolf's and Pitama-kan's great herd, and I caught one of them, led him into the fort and saddled him.

At breakfast Abbott said, "I see you have saddled your pinto runner for the hunt."

"Yes," I answered.

"Ha! He is a good horse, a swift runner," said Tsistsaki. "With him you will be sure to kill some fat meat for us."

At the words shame came to me. I looked down at my plate and felt my face turn red. I said to myself that I would not take Is-spai-u. I hoped that they had not noticed my embarrassment. I cast a stealthy glance at my almost-mother and then another at Abbott. Both were giving their whole attention to their food. I rose from the table and, seizing my rifle and my ammunition, hurried across the court to the pinto, mounted him and rode out through the wide gate of the fort.

In the distance I could see White Wolf's forty lodges of hunters, a long line of mounted men and women and children, led travois-horses, pack-horses and band after band of loose horses strung out upon the up-river trail. I quickened my pace to overtake them and passed the outer bounds of the great camp. Again I was tempted to take Is-spai-u. For a moment or two I fought it; then I brought my horse to an unwilling stand. "I will take Is-spai-u!" I said and turned back to the fort. "Under the protection of all those warrior hunters no harm can possibly come to him!"

A little way from the fort I tied the pinto to some brush and went straight to the stable and led out the prancing, nervous horse.

As I passed our quarters Abbott came out and said to me, "You are taking Is-spai-u to water? I was just going to do that."

I could not speak. My heart was beating fast. I nodded and hurried on straight to the river. Of course I was going to water the horse. That was no lie; but what a lie I was acting! As I led the animal back up the steep bank to the flat fear came to me. I took the well-worn path to the gate of the fort, and then —

"No! I will not take him back to the stable!" I said to myself. "I've just got to have some good buffalo runs with him!"

A few minutes later, riding Is-spai-u and leading the pinto, I was hurrying to overtake the caravan.

Now imagine me lying there on my couch, so sick at heart that I heard not a word of what was being said.

Suddenly the mighty voice of Bull's Plume aroused me. "We have to avenge our dead," he roared. "We have to recover our fast buffalo runners; to-morrow I shall lead a war party upon the trail of this enemy."

"And I go with you!" I cried. "I have to recover Is-spai-u. I just have to do that!"

White Wolf gave me a pitying look and shook his head. Then, turning to Bull's Plume, he said, "Friend, we here are too few to make up a war party; we cannot strike out after the enemy and leave our women and children to be killed by some other enemy that may come this way. The thing for us to do is this: some of us try to learn who the raiders of our camp are, and others of us go back to our people to call out a large party to take their trail."

"Well said! Wise advice!" old Red Eagle exclaimed. "I further propose that we ask the chiefs to move the whole camp out here. Day after day the people sit there in idleness, eating their stores of dried meat, waiting for the coming of Far Thunder with the trade goods that we so much need. It will be a long time, maybe still a whole moon, before the watchers at the fort discover the far downriver smoke of his fireboat. The people will be much better off out here at the foot of the mountains, where game is plentiful."

"Sacred man, we take your words," White

Wolf told him. Then, knocking the ashes from the smoked-out pipe, he exclaimed, "See, there! Now it is all burned up!"

I had no sleep that night. The ceaseless wailing of the widowed and of the fatherless were fit accompaniment to my own sad thoughts. How I hated myself for disobeying my uncle and losing his wonderful buffalo horse! "No; unless I can recover Is-spai-u I can never face my Uncle Wesley again," I said to myself many times before morning broke.

With the first gray light of day I aroused White Wolf and Pitamakan, and we took up our weapons and went out. Some men were ahead of us; others were just leaving their lodges. We scattered up and down the valley and out on the plain and found here and there bands of our horses quietly grazing. It was as White Wolf had guessed; the raiders had had no use for our common stock; they were getting Is-spai-u and our other buffalo runners out of our country as fast as they could.

The sky was heavily overcast, and we had

scarcely caught horses enough to take the trail of the enemy and try to determine who they were before a cloudburst broke upon us. Within five minutes every coulee coming into the valley from the plains was a roaring torrent of yellow, foaming water; the trail of the enemy was completely obliterated. The Musselshell was rapidly rising and widening and inundating the bottom lands; we had to help the women move camp to higher ground; and, though we worked fast, the flood bore away the belongings of several families. In bitterness of heart men and women here and there were crying out that the gods had forsaken us.

Regardless of the storm, White Wolf was shouting for volunteers to go with the council's message to the chiefs of the great camp at the fort. Pitamakan and I answered the call and were soon mounted and upon our way. Our horses had to splash through mud and water that in places was more than knee-deep.

Long before noon the storm passed as suddenly as it had come, and the sun shone warm upon us;

but the going was bad, and we did not arrive at the mouth of the river until late in the afternoon. Pitamakan went to the lodges of the chiefs with White Wolf's message; and I, slumped down in my saddle, rode slowly through the gateway of the fort. One of the *engagés* had noticed my approach and given word. From our quarters Tsistsaki came running across the court to meet me, and Abbott, followed by some of our men and their women, also appeared.

"Oh, my son!" Tsistsaki cried, looking quickly up at me with drawn face and wide, staring eyes. "Something terrible has happened to you!"

"Yes!" I answered. "The very worst! The enemy stole Is-spai-u from me last night!" I faltered and bit my lips hard to keep from crying.

With a gasp my almost-mother threw up her hands and began to cry.

"Thomas Fox," said Abbott, frowning sternly, "you surely have done it now! I'm to blame, too, for I should have taken your trail yesterday to bring Is-spai-u back safe to his stable. But I could n't get away; we had a big trade yesterday, and again this morning. Well, I should n't like to be in your place when you face your uncle!"

"I'm not going to face him until I have Is-spai-u close behind me," I told him. "A big war party is to go out after the enemy, and I go with it. I will recover the horse!"

I followed my almost-mother into our quarters, and while she listlessly began preparing our evening meal I threw myself down into my uncle's buffalo-hide chair by the comfortable blaze in the adobe fireplace.

CHAPTER II

IN WHICH THE SACRED FAST BEGINS

SOON Abbott came in, but as he drew up in front of the fire he said not a word to me. Then just as Tsistsaki was placing the food upon the table, Pitamakan came happily humming a war song. We drew up to the table.

"What a quick-minded chief Big Lake is!" Pitamakan exclaimed. "I had no more than given my father's message than he had made his decision about it. The last of my words were not out of my mouth when he began telling the camp crier to order the people to prepare to move camp in the early morning; then he turned to Bull-Turns-Around and told him to organize a war party to avenge the wrongs the enemy have done us."

"I am glad that Bull-Turns-Around is to be our leader," I said. "I think that I would rather follow him than any other warrior of the Pikuni."

At that I saw Pitamakan give my almost-mother

a queer look of understanding, which she answered by a sad nod of her head.

"What is it?" I cried impulsively. "Tell me. What is it that you two are hiding from me?"

"My son, we are hiding nothing from you," she answered. "You must know, without our telling you, that neither Bull-Turns-Around nor any other chief will allow you to take the war trail."

"I do not know. Have n't I lost Is-spai-u? Why should I be refused the opportunity to get him back from the enemy?" I impatiently asked.

"For the very good reason that you have never taken your vision fast. No one may go with a war party against the enemy until he has endured his fast and thereby obtained a sacred helper," Pitamakan explained.

"But I am different. I have already met and fought enemies — " I began.

"Not with a war party," said Tsistsaki.

"Ha! I am going straight to Bull-Turns-Around and see about this. I know he will let me join his party!" I cried and pushed back from the table, snatched my cap, and ran off into camp and straight to the warrior's lodge.

Hurriedly entering, trembling with excitement, I interrupted a council he was having with a large circle of his men. All stared at me as I knelt close to the doorway; some darkly frowned. I felt very small, very insignificant, there in the presence of those great warriors.

But I at once took heart when Bull-Turns-Around said to me in a kind, soothing voice, "Yes, my son! What can we do for you?"

"Much! Oh, very much!" I cried across the circle to him. "Against my uncle's orders I stole Is-spai-u away from the fort to go with White Wolf and run buffalo. Last night the enemy raiders got him. O chief, as you love your wives and your children, I beg you to let me join your war party! I must recover that wonderful horse! You know that I am no coward — that I have already fought our enemies. Let me go with you as your pipe-bearer, if as nothing more."

A long silence followed my plea. I saw that none

of the gathering was now scowling at me; all were gazing at the fire in deep thought.

Then the chief turned to a noted sun priest sitting upon his right, and said, "Tail Feathers, favored of the sun, you give our young friend our answer to his plea."

"Otahtoyi, my son," the old man said to me, "long have we watched you growing up among us, becoming one of us, and we are very proud that you are one of us. We know that you are brave and of kind and generous heart. Nevertheless, my son, the request that you make we must refuse to grant, not because we fear that you would not be right in the front of the battle, but because, having never obtained the favor of the gods by fasting and prayer, you would endanger the very lives of those with whom you took the war trail. War, my son, is not alone a matter of endurance and bravery; it is an undertaking that requires constant prayer and sacrifice by every member of the party, and you can make neither prayer nor sacrifice, that the gods will heed until you have by lone, long fasting obtained their favor. There! My son, that is the only answer which we can give you, and sorry I am to say it."

I turned and looked questioningly at the war chief.

"Yes, my son," he said, "Tail Feathers' words are our words. But do not lose heart. Take courage! If the gods help us, we shall find Is-spai-u and return him to you."

Well I knew that it would be useless for me to make another plea; a decision of a war council was never reversed. I went sadly home and again sat before the fire. My companions knew by the expression of my face what answer I had received, and though they glanced often at me they did not question me.

"Pitamakan, almost-brother," I said after some thought, "it was as you said it would be. Bull-Turns-Around will not let me join his party because I have not had my sacred fast. But I can't remain here or in camp, waiting for him and his men to find Is-spai-u and bring him back to me.

They may never find him. Come you with me in quest of him."

"Of course I will go with you — "

"Oh, good! I knew that you would!" I broke in.

"But not until you have had your sacred fast," he concluded.

"I have long wanted you to endure it!" cried Tsistsaki.

I looked across the hearth at Abbott.

"Do it!" he said emphatically. "Because why? It will make you solid forever with all the Blackfeet tribes and with the Gros Ventres as well. And believe me, boy, it will be a worthwhile experience for you; by the time you have finished the fast you will know a lot more about the animals of this country than you could otherwise learn in a whole lifetime."

He spoke in English, and Tsistsaki, who understood it well, but who never spoke it, turned upon him and in her own tongue reproachfully cried, "O Otsimi (Sorrel Horse)! Is that all you can say in favor of my son's enduring a fast? Oh, I fear you have become an unbeliever! How, think you, have you survived all the dangers that you have faced these many summers and winters back? Would you be here now if you had not endured a fast and thereby obtained the favor of the gods?"

Poor Abbott! He turned red of face and shifted uneasily in his chair and knew not what to reply. It was news to me that he had undergone a sacred fast in his younger days and did not want me to know it. I covered his embarrassment.

"Almost-brother, almost-brother!" I cried. "I will do as you advise. But where shall I endure the fast?"

"Let my father or old Red Eagle decide that," said Pitamakan.

By eight o'clock the next morning the caravan of the Pikuni, miles long, was moving steadily up the valley of the Musselshell. Pitamakan and I with a number of clan chiefs and warriors passed it and rode swiftly on ahead and at about four o'clock arrived at White Wolf's camp. The great body of the people did not come in until so late that they barely had time to set up their lodges and gather fuel before night settled down upon the valley.

White Wolf had news for us. Hard as had been the cloudburst of the previous day, it had not entirely washed out the trail of the enemy; in several places up the river were footprints of horses. The general opinion was that the raiders were Crows, and that they were fleeing south as fast as they could ride to the protection of their tribe somewhere on Elk River — the Yellowstone — or south of it in the vast stretch of plains and mountain country that the River Crows and their brother tribe, the Mountain Crows, owned. In the past two years war parties from those two tribes had been most persistent of all in attempting to take Is-spai-u from us. Always we had outfought and outwitted them until now through my own fault they at last had the animal in their possession. How I hated myself that evening! The food that was passed to me tasted bitter.

During the day scouts had found to the west of camp buffaloes as numerous as the grass and countless bands of other game at the foot of the Moc-casin Mountains. Early in the evening the chiefs counseled together and decided that we should move camp to the extreme head of It-Crushed-Them Creek instead of to the farther-off slope of the Snow Mountains; and while they counseled and smoked Bull-Turns-Around and his hundred war-riors gathered in three sweat lodges where, in the dense steam rising from the water-sprinkled, red-hot rocks, Red Eagle, Tail Feathers, and another sun priest earnestly prayed the gods to preserve them from all danger and to give them success in their undertaking. Some time before midnight I heard the war chief call his men together and heard the soft thudding of their moccasined feet as they filed past our lodge.

On the following day we moved west to the head of It-Crushed-Them Creek. The rolling plain was fairly teeming with buffaloes and antelopes, and when we turned up the gently rising slope of the mountains to make camp in a wide cottonwood grove at the head of the creek, band after band of

elks and deer fled at our approach. All the afternoon first one group of hunters, then another, had
circled out from the long caravan and had returned
with all the meat their horses could carry. As the
sun went down there was a vast hum of happy talk
and laughter, of drumming and singing and of
dancing from one end of the great camp to the
other, except in three or four lodges where women
and children unceasingly wailed the names of their
loved ones who had been killed in the recent raid.

During the day Pitamakan had told White
Wolf and Red Eagle, the sun priest, about my
determination to endure a sacred fast, and now
after the evening meal the two men talked with
me about it.

"Otahtoyi, my son," White Wolf said to me,
"we are very glad that you are going out to fast
and thus obtain the favor of the gods. Now, in
the days of my youth we happened to be encamped
right where we are to-night when the time came for
me to fast, and I chose a place straight west from
here in which to endure it. I advise you to make it

your fasting place. Follow the foot of the mountain slope, and you will come to an outstanding, cliff-faced butte, close to the foot of which is a deep, clear spring. To that spring come many of the children of the plains, and from the heights above the mountain children trail down to it to quench their thirst; you will, of course, pray to them all for help, and without doubt one or another of them will pity you and give you the vision that you seek. Not far from the spring, low down on the face of the cliff, you will find a narrow rock shelf with a lone pine tree standing on it. I lay right under the tree and had a buffalo bull's skull for a pillow. I advise you to lie there."

"I shall go there," I said.

"That is good. You will come to my lodge early in the morning for your instructions," old Red Eagle replied and, smiling, arose and went his way home.

For me alone Red Eagle got out his thunder medicine pipe the next morning and with his helpers went through the whole ceremony of it.

First he painted my face and hands with red, Sun's favorite and sacred color; then he prayed the sky gods and the gods of the earth, the air and the water to give me a good vision; finally he gave me my instructions. I was not to eat food of any kind; I could drink water only after sundown and before sunrise. I was not to wash the sacred paint from my face and hands until I had completed my fast. During my waking hours I was to pray to the gods and to each of the animals that I saw to become my helper, my lifetime shield from all dangers.

I went forth from the lodge with a strange feeling of elation and of reverence for my friends' absolute faith in their gods. I did not ask myself how fully I shared their faith. I had seen many apparently direct answers to their prayers and sacrifices, and only a few evenings before, close following Sun's painting himself, death and heavy loss had come upon us. I was determined to carry out the old medicine man's instructions in every detail. If I leaned toward the faith of the Blackfeet, I must not be blamed; I had known it from childhood days up to this time of my maturing youth. My early childhood days in far-away St. Louis and the teachings of father and of mother, both of whom were taken from me by the dreadful smallpox plague, were like a misty dream.

While Pitamakan and I caught and saddled two of our horses, the women brought out from our lodge the few things that I should need during my fast — two buffalo robes and two blankets for my couch, my rifle, my ammunition, and my knife. We tied the bedding behind our saddles, mounted and struck out through camp to the west just as the camp crier, by order of Big Lake and his council of clan chiefs, was warning the people not to hunt or to travel anywhere near the outstanding, cliff-faced butte during the time that I was there enduring my sacred fast.

About six miles from camp we arrived at our destination. We dismounted at the cliff, and I climbed up on the rock shelf under the lone pine tree and saw the buffalo skull that White Wolf had used for a pillow during his fast there long ago; it was yellowed and stained green with age. Pitamakan passed up my bedding and rifle, took the lead rope of my horse, and got into his saddle.

"I may as well turn right back for home," he said. "I pray that you may have a powerful vision and obtain a powerful sacred helper in this place."

"I shall do all I can; it rests with the gods," I answered and slumped down upon the shelf and dazedly watched him ride out of sight. I felt that I had been in a daze all day. The danger of my position suddenly came to me, and I almost sprang up to shout to Pitamakan to come back for me, but I could not do it; the disgrace would be more than I could bear.

"Now that you have undertaken this fast you must finish it," I said to myself; and with that I turned and brushed off the stones and the sticks that time had deposited under the tree, carefully made my soft robe bed, placed a folded blanket upon the buffalo skull for a pillow, and lay down, facing the spring about fifty yards down the slope from me. It was in a bare, gravelly depression, and was ten or twelve feet in diameter and very deep. A small stream trickled from it and was soon absorbed by the thirsty plain. Game trails radiated from it in all directions. Watching them, and every moment expecting to see game come filing along to the water, I soon fell asleep.

When I awoke night had come, and a full moon was well up in the eastern sky. I was very hungry and very thirsty. I looked down at the spring and saw a small band of cow elks crowding round it, a few with newborn young snuggling at their sides.

"Haiyu! Skim ponokahks! Kimoket! Nok-spumoket! (O female elks, pity me! Do help me!)" I prayed them in a whisper.

Then while I watched them I again fell asleep and did not wake until the first light of coming day tinged the eastern sky.

A band of twenty-five or thirty buffaloes, all cows and most of them with funny little red calves at their sides, were now coming in single file up to the spring; an exceptionally large cow with twin calves led them. As was ever the case at that time of year, numbers of small blackbirds — or, as the Blackfeet called them, "ksi-ni-u," buffalo birds — accompanied the buffaloes. It was not an uncommon sight to see four or five of them contentedly riding along upon the back of a cow, all on the watch for the stinging flies, the gnats and the mosquitoes that pestered the great beasts, and darting into the air and catching them and fluttering back to their perches. The favorite feeding places for the small black gnats was the tender, bare eyelid of the buffalo, and frequently a bird would cling to the coarse hair above an eye and protect it from the attacks of the enemy. The buffaloes were grateful to the birds for that service, the Blackfeet said, and in return permitted them to build nests and rear their young deep down in the long thick hair that crowned their massive heads.

There was much crowding and angry snorting when the buffaloes gathered at the little spring, and the milder animals gave way to the aggressive ones and meekly stood back and drank last. When all had quenched their thirst they one by one lay down in a circle round the spring, and their calves lay well within the circle.

From far off round the butte there came to me the cry of a lone wolf, a long-drawn-out, melancholy, slowly rising and falling howl that seemed to be burdened with all the woes of the world. Sad though it was, I loved to listen to it. I agreed with my Blackfeet people when they said that the howling of wolves was more pleasant to the ears than even the quavering cries of sandhill cranes, the trumpeting of swans, or the calling of gray geese winging their way over the great plains.

Again the lone wolf howled, and others, some very near, some so far away that I could no more than hear them, answered. I knew, of course, that he was the leader of a band, and that he was calling his comrades to gather for a hunt.

I thought that wolves might come my way, and in the course of a half-hour or so they did come, thirteen of them upon the trail leading from the east to the spring. The leader, a very large, cream-white male, evidently had the morning hunt all planned; he led his band at a steady trot, stopping not once to sniff at the bunches of sage growing here and there at the sides of the trail. His followers were of varying shades of gray and black. Their long, fluffy coats, which reached high above their shoulders, quivered in time with their footsteps; they held their round, thick-furred tails at a graceful drooping angle from their bodies; their broad heads gave evidence of their great intelligence. They were, the Blackfeet said, the wisest and the most successful hunters in all the world.

Now when the old white leader came to the rim of the depression in which the spring lay he saw the buffaloes lying round it and stopped short, and his followers, flanking him upon either side and crowding up close behind him, also came to a stop, all standing as motionless as so many statues.

Not so the buffaloes. A cow lying to the west of the spring discovered the enemy as they came to a halt and, loudly snorting, sprang to her feet with wonderful agility for so large and unwieldy an animal and with lowered head faced them. Her hair bristled forward like that of an angry dog. The other cows all sprang up and crowded into a close-packed mass behind her. The little calves had got upon their feet more quickly than their mothers, and in their fright several of them started to run straight away from the band; but they made only a few leaps and came scurrying back and darted under their mothers' bellies and disappeared from sight.

The wolves now relaxed the tense posture into which they had frozen at sight of the buffaloes; they shifted their feet uneasily and looked at one another and down at the little herd, and presently, as if the old white leader had ordered them to do so, several of them started at a slow walk to circle the herd — at a very respectful distance, however. The leader then sat down on his haunches while the rest of his followers remained standing a short distance behind him.

In hope, doubtless, of finding a sleeping calf, the circling scouts pursued a zigzag course from one clump of sagebrush to another; and those that took the upper side of the slope passed within fifty feet of me. As they went round, some of the cows kept turning their heads toward them, and soon the little herd had shaped itself into a circling wall of menacing, sharp-horned heads alight with gleaming eyes. The wolves were wise with the experiences of their ancestors — experiences accumulated through countless years; they knew that an attack upon the herd would result in their being gored to death, that it would be impossible for them to stampede the courageous mothers and pull down their young.

The scouts in the lead had completely circled the herd; the others stopped here and there round it. All looked back at their old leader, who presently arose and started off at a trot. As he passed below the buffaloes he disdained even to give them a glance and went round the butte with his followers.

The buffaloes remained in close formation for a

long time after the wolves had gone; then with their calves close at their sides or trailing right at their heels they started off down the slope at a brisk walk and went far out upon the plain before scattering over it to graze.

I had called upon the wolves and the buffaloes — or rather upon their far-back ancestors — for help, whispering my prayers word for word as old Red Eagle had taught me them. I now realized that I was partly exposed to the sharp eyes of all visitors to the spring; so I got up and broke a large, spreading branch from the pine tree, laid it between my couch and the outer edge of the shelf and found with satisfaction that it was all the screen I needed.

I had no more than lain down when, looking out through the green tufts of needles, I saw the old white wolf and his followers loping swiftly back round the butte toward the spring. Their tails were no longer outstretched; they kept looking back over their shoulders as they ran, and I knew that they were fleeing from the one thing that they

43

feared — man. They sped down into the depression of the spring and up its eastern slope and were gone. Then, looking to the west, I saw a war party coming in single file round the shoulder of the butte. I counted forty-three men. There was no chance that they were from one of our Blackfeet tribes, for they carried no shields and no fringed and painted parfleche cylinders containing war bonnet and war clothes; they were from some enemy tribe. I flattened down close upon my couch behind the screen of pine branch and called softly upon Sun to protect me.

CHAPTER III

IN WHICH A COUGAR CLIMBS THE SLOPE

A S the enemy came nearer I saw that several of them wore robes of tanned elk skins, and one a robe of the white mountain goat; they were, then, from some West Side tribe. They were all short men with heavy bodies and coarse features. Their frowzy, short hair seemed never to have been combed and braided. All were armed with bows and arrows, but only three or four of them carried guns. They were obviously members of one of the Snake tribes, a numerous people who lived at the headwaters of the Snake River and on the Columbia. I knew only too well what my fate would be if they should see me!

On they came down the slope to the spring, gathered round it, knelt and drank. One of them turned and looked up at the cliff, apparently at the very shelf on which I lay. He said something to his companions, and at the same time pointed

45

straight toward me. Was he saying to them that the big pine branch could not have broken of its own weight? The stub of it, snow-white and sound through and through, was proof enough of that.

I groaned aloud. Why had I not daubed the break with moistened earth? Was my innocent screen to be the cause of my death? Cold sweat broke out on me.

Three or four of the man's companions turned and looked up where he was pointing, and I took a firmer grip on my rifle. If they started up toward me, I would shoot the leader, spring from the shelf and run. I should have a lead of fifty yards; there was a bare chance that their arrows and bullets would not touch me, and, if they failed to hit me, I could perhaps outrun them. I made a silent, agonized appeal for help. Then, as if in answer to my prayer, something happened to divert their attention from my hiding-place. With a loud exclamation a man on the lower side of the circle pointed to the plain where, six or eight miles to the northeast, a large herd of buffaloes was surging swiftly out from the pineclad breaks of It-Crushed-Them Creek. Fleeing game — a great herd of it — meant only one thing: the presence of man. Long and silently my enemies watched the wide black mass of animals run with never-slackening speed on into the west until they disappeared behind a group of flat-topped, pineclad buttes. No horsemen appeared to pursue them, but I knew that some of our hunters, probably two or three men setting traps for beaver along the creek, had frightened them. How glad I was that a party of our buffalo runners had not followed at the tail of the herd! The enemies at the spring would at once have inferred that our camp was not far off; and of course a camp, near which they could waylay straggling hunters and raid the herds of horses, was what they sought. As no hunters followed the buffaloes, they reasoned, of course, that a traveling war party had frightened the animals; and, judging from what I knew of the Snakes, I felt sure that a war party was something they would do their best to avoid.

They had a short, excited consultation. Then, crouching low and without another glance in my direction, they began one after another to go slowly back along the game trail that they had followed to the spring. My tense muscles relaxed; I felt suddenly weak. I felt with awe that the gods had saved me from a great danger.

I cannot be blamed for my faith in the Indian gods in those far-away days of my youth; my beliefs were the inevitable result of my life among the Indians. As children in civilized homes unquestioningly accept the teachings of their elders, so I accepted the teachings of Tsistsaki, my almost-mother, and of my dear Blackfeet friends and counselors.

I was now hungry, and my throat was parched, but I could not drink from the cool, deep spring until the sun went down! I resolutely put my hunger and thirst from my mind and thought of other things. Should I actually have a vision here on the rock shelf, I wondered. And if I did have one, what ancient animal or bird would appear and offer to become my sacred, lifelong helper? As I thought about the little band of cows and calves that had come to the spring to drink and rest, there came to my mind strange tales that I had heard of the buffaloes, particularly the legend of the Four Bulls, which was a favorite of the Blackfeet medicine men. Here it is:

In the days when the Blackfeet had the great plains wholly to themselves and war was unknown, a man one morning told his wives to pack the dogs. When all was ready he took the lead, and they started out upon discovery to see new country. One evening, as they sat by their little lodge fire, they heard heavy, slow footsteps approaching; then the door was thrust aside, and four elegantly dressed young men came in. The hunter welcomed them, gave them seats of honor at the back of the lodge, and had his women set food before them. In answer to his questions, they said that they were from a far camp of people and were merely traveling to see the country. They did not tarry long after they had eaten food and smoked the pipe of peace, but they promised to come again. When the visitors went off into the night, the hunter and his wives wondered why they stepped so heavily.

On the following evening the man and his wives heard again the sound of heavy walking on the dry ground, and again the four strangers entered the lodge. That time they remained until nearly midnight; and when the talk turned to sacred things they said that they had great favor with Sun. They taught their host some of their sacred prayers and songs.

Four nights in all the strangers visited the hunter, teaching him their way of worshiping Sun and winning his favor; but on the last night, after they had been some time in the lodge, there came a light fall of snow, which for some reason seemed to disturb them. They kept looking at one another and fidgeting in their seats, and at last they told the hunter that they had taught him all the sacred rites they knew, and that they had decided to resume their travels. They filed out of the lodge, and for the last time the little family heard the sound of their heavy retreating footsteps. One of the wives again remarked that it was strange that active young men should make so much noise when they walked.

Presently she left the lodge and soon after shrieked to her man to come to her. They all rushed outside and found her pointing down into the snow. "Just look at the tracks of our departed visitors!" she cried.

They stared down at them and could hardly believe their eyes, for what they saw were unmistakably the tracks of buffalo bulls.

One of the wives burst into tears. "Oh, misfortune, death, perhaps, is upon us!" she cried.

"Hush, woman! Dry your tears and be glad," the man commanded. "Don't you realize that our visitors are our friends, that they have earnestly, patiently taught me all the rites of their wonderful buffalo medicine? Oh, the gods are good to us! Let us rejoice! Let us rejoice!"

Thus it was that in the long ago the Blackfeet

got the buffalo medicine. For centuries it was transmitted from one to another. Its symbols — a huge red-mouthed, red-hearted black buffalo bull and a cow — were painted one on the right side and one on the left side of the lodge of the one who had the sacred learning. Now old Lone Man had it. How many times had I heard him, assisted by brother medicine men and by his women, singing the weird songs of the Four Bulls! One song I especially loved, it was so slow and deep and sonorous, and so clearly imitated the stately, deliberate movements of a lone old bull. If I was to have a vision I hoped that a buffalo would appear and offer to become my helper and protector.

I slept again, and that time I had a dream. But it was indistinct; all that I could remember of it when I awoke was that it had to do with buffaloes and a wind-swept snowy plain.

The sun now was low in the west. Even before I opened my eyes I realized that I was hungry and thirsty. Three bighorn rams had come down from the rocky heights above me and were drinking at the spring. I had only to poke my rifle out through the screen, kill one of them and build a fire, and I would soon be feasting upon the best of meat. I was greatly tempted, but I remembered in time old Red Eagle's instructions:

"You have now vowed to endure your sacred fast. In no circumstances except one — that you are attacked by an enemy — may you leave your place of retirement or break your fast for four nights and four days, the number sacred to Sun. Then if you have had no vision, if you feel that your fasting place has not been well chosen, you may kill something and eat and choose another fasting-place; or you may come home and later try again to find a sacred helper."

Thinking it over, I said to myself that for the specified time, or for twice as long if necessary, I would remain where I was and carry out my instructions to the last detail.

As the three bighorn rams turned away from the spring, I sent my silent prayer out to them for help. They paused and looked up toward me, moved on, and climbed the steep butte to the east of the cliff. Long after they had passed out of sight, I could hear the tinkling of the fragments of rock that they dislodged.

From above, a Clarke's crow, raucously calling, fluttered into the top of the pine tree. I made a slight movement, and the bird hopped down from limb to limb, scolding so loud and so incessantly that three or four of his kind soon joined him and added their scoldings to his. They hopped nervously about in the branches, upward or downward, and frequently paused to cock their heads at me and then chatter all the louder. I wished they would go away; nevertheless, I addressed to them my prayer for help.

In watching the crows I had for some time neglected to look down at the spring. I now turned my eyes toward it, and, lo! to the west of it stood a large cougar staring up in my direction with its big, cold, yellow eyes. Its long tail was writhing like a dying snake; its flexible nose was sniffing the air. Thus it stood for several moments; then it cautiously stepped on toward the spring, stopped short, and, squatting on its haunches, again stared up at the shelf on which I lay. It was wondering what the crows had found there to excite them to such furious cries of protest. Three or four times the great cat looked down at the spring and licked its jaws. Finally it moved on toward the water, but after a few steps it stood still again and again stared up at the scolding crows. Its inquisitiveness was greater than its thirst. With a last look at the spring it began slowly to climb the slope, hesitantly placing one foot before another and crouching so low that its belly almost swept the ground.

Now, I was not at all afraid of the cougar. All our hunters were agreed that it was the most cowardly of all the carnivorous animals. As an old friend of mine once put it, "There is just one place where cougars climb trees to lie in wait for people, or where they trail them and spring upon their backs; that place is round the barroom stove in the winter-time!"

All the same, I did not intend that the cougar

should spring up and land on me, perhaps with its sharp claws in my face. Through the shelter of the screen I watched him sneak up the slope until the overhang of the shelf hid him from me. I waited for him to come close, and then, suddenly leaning out, I half blew, half hissed at him. At the moment he was shuffling his feet as if to jump; instead of leaping upward, he twisted sidewise and went into the air and, snarling and spitting, sailed off down the slope for fully thirty feet before he struck the ground, and then went leaping on and on to the east and was soon gone from sight.

I had not thought to pray for help! "O great killer of deer," I called out after his vanishing form, "pity me, help me to get what I seek."

Some blue grouse — all males — now came to the spring and drank. A lone coyote came and frightened them away. From all directions fluttered the small birds for their evening sup of water. Then in succession came elks, deer, two wolves, and finally a lone bull moose, a two-year-old, pot-bellied and still thin of flesh. Its new antlers still

in the velvet were no longer than my two hands. To all those birds and animals that came and drank and went their various ways I addressed my plea for help.

The sun dropped behind the mountains; my own time to drink had come. I hurried down to the spring and took my fill of the clear, cold water. As I retraced my steps to my resting place, I realized that my hunger was gone and that I had wonderful lightness and strength of body. I went up the steep slope as easily as if it were level ground.

I now slept for a while. When I awoke the moon was shining in my face, and I saw by the position of the Seven Persons that the time was near midnight. I had had a hazy dream of a wintry plain on which the snow lay deep. Snow was falling. A lone buffalo, coated with snow, with its breath rising in clouds of steam, was feeding there, pawing and thrusting its huge head deep into the snow to get at the short grass underneath. I, afoot, was trying to approach it. The snow was heavy and almost thigh-deep, and I was nearly exhausted.

I wondered whether I should have strength to wade to the animal's trail, when I should have easier going. Wearily and still more wearily I pressed on, and then suddenly — nothing more! How I wished that my dream had been clearer, that it had come to a definite and satisfactory end!

But what was that which came to my ears? Unmistakably the low murmur of human voices! On the edge of the cliff above me men were talking. I grasped my rifle and sat up to hear more clearly; my heart beat fast. Then rocks began to tinkle down the steep mountain slope as if they had been dislodged by the passing of many feet. Lying down, I looked through my screen of pine and soon saw men leave the foot of the steep, hurry to the spring and throw themselves flat on the ground to drink. They were the men whom I had seen come there before, drink and then sneak back to the west. But since then they had been up on the mountain and from its heights had undoubtedly seen the great camp of my people.

One by one they arose from their drinking and

struck off to the east straight toward the camp. In my distress I bit my lips to keep from groaning aloud. I wanted to circle past them, run on and warn my people of their coming. But old Red Eagle had told me in no circumstances to leave my fasting place for at least four days and four nights, unless I should get my sacred vision before that time, or unless an enemy attacked me. "I cannot go; I must remain right here," I said to myself. I tried to comfort myself with the thought that the enemy were only forty-three poorly armed Snakes. Undoubtedly they would round up the first band of horses they came to and hurry west with their plunder. By the time they had stolen the horses morning would be near; my people would soon be on their trail and would easily overtake and kill them all. How hard I tried to convince myself that that was exactly what would happen! But I could not forget another possibility; during the coming day the enemy might lie in wait for stray hunters, ambush them, and the following evening raid our herds and get safe away on the trail to their distant home. Once in my distress I sprang from my shelf, ran a hundred yards toward home and then stopped short. How often it had been impressed on me that to disregard a medicine man's instructions meant some terrible misfortune to him as well as to the breaker of his law! I returned slowly to my resting place and lay down again. Although my mind was in great turmoil, I sank almost at once into a heavy dreamless sleep.

I awoke soon after sunrise — too late for my morning drink at the spring. Sitting up, I stared off to the east and north and west as far as I could see, but no riders were in sight. Everywhere bands of buffalo and antelope were peacefully grazing in the cool of the morning. What of the war party? Had they raided some of our herds? Were they in hiding near our camp? How I wished I knew! All day long I kept anxious watch on the great plains; all day long came the usual birds and animals to the spring — to all of whom I prayed for help. Night came, and I went down to the spring and drank. Hunger had wholly left me. I was not thirsty. I returned to my couch and slept all through the night, awakening in time to drink before sunrise.

I had no sooner got back from the spring to my couch than the deer and the elks began to come for their morning drink; then came the birds and the smaller animals, among which were several foxes and two skunks. I called on them all for help. My friends the hunting pack of wolves had not reappeared, but now soon after sunrise a lone wolf began howling somewhere off to the northwest; others of his kind, some near, some so far away that I could barely hear them, answered him in a gradually swelling chorus. The howling ceased; for fifteen or twenty minutes all was silent. Then near by and straight to the east the lone wolf howled again. At once the air fairly vibrated with long-drawn-out, melancholy wails. It was, I believed, the old white leader gathering his pack for the hunt.

After an hour or more had passed, I concluded that the wolves had gone down into the timbered breaks of It-Crushed-Them Creek in quest of meat. Then from round the west shoulder of the butte came a lone buffalo bull. He was slowly and painfully limping along the deeply worn game trail to the spring. He stopped frequently to hold up his right forefoot and rest. When he walked he scarcely touched it to the ground, but, supporting himself on his sound left foreleg, went lunging forward. His flanks heaved with exertion.

As he came nearer I saw that he was in the prime of life, a bull not more than five or six years old. His black, curved horns were fully grown, sharp and perfect in point; battles and mad gougings into cutbanks had not yet marred them. Moreover, he was fat; his new summer growth of hair was smooth and lustrous; only here and there along his hump a few faded, tattered shreds of his winter coat still clung. Evidently he had lamed himself by stepping on a sharp stick or fragment of rock, which had penetrated his foot. As soon as I saw him I thought of my dream of the lone bull on the wintry plain, and in a whisper I cried out to him,

"O lone lame bull, pity me! Ask your buffalo-men ancestors to help me!"

Arriving at the spring, the bull drank long and deep, raised his dripping muzzle and long beard and heaved a great sigh of satisfaction and drank again and again until he could hold no more. Then he turned and began to limp off down the slope. At that moment, happening to look off to my right, I saw the wolves, the same pack I had seen before. They were ranged along the edge of the slope that ran down to the spring. The old white leader was standing somewhat in advance and as motionless as a rock; all of them were intently watching the limping bull. They watched him hungrily, with their heavy ears set stiffly forward, and their heads held low on outstretched necks.

I counted seventeen. The pack had increased by four. Presently the old white leader turned his head and looked back at his followers. That look was his order to charge. Away they went down the slope, with him in the lead. Their sharp claws sent the gravelly earth flying behind them.

The bull, as well as I, heard the hissing of the gravel and well knew what it meant. He stopped short, but before he could turn around, the pack was upon him. Up went his short, tufted tail; he humped his back, lowered his great head and snorted. He was powerfully aggressive in his anger, and he seemed to be proof against the attack of all the wolves of the plains.

The old white leader and all but four of his pack went to the front of the bull and kept circling past him and snapping at his nose as they shot through the air. They did not go close enough to touch it, and in vain he kept thrusting at them with his sharp horns. Meanwhile the four were swiftly circling nearer and nearer behind him, until at last one of them in passing made a lightninglike snap at his left leg and tore it badly just above the hoofs. With both feet the bull kicked back, but since he had only one sound forefoot he almost lost his balance in doing so. But his kick struck the next one of the passing wolves fair in the side and knocked it high into the air. With a hard thud it struck the ground, got up and staggered farther away and lay down. Its three mates continued to circle at their deadly work, snapping at the bull's heels and tearing them now and then until both were red with blood.

CHAPTER IV

IN WHICH NO RUNNER BRINGS WORD OF IS–SPAI–U

THE wolves' harrying that bull was the cruelest sight I had ever seen; but I knew that worse was coming. I was burning with anger at the pack; I had only to stand up and shout to have them go even faster than they had come. Yet I could not do it, for old Red Eagle had told me that in no circumstances was I to interfere with the animals and the birds that I saw; and I had to obey his orders. I tried to excuse my failure to end the cruel tragedy by saying that it was not for me to interfere. Who was I to question the inexorable laws of nature? Had not the Great Maker fashioned the wolves for the very work that they were doing?

Two wolves came from the front to aid the three that were circling and snapping at the heels of the bull. In vain he kicked out, now with one hoof, now with the other; the great tendon of his left

66

leg was soon severed, and the leg hung useless. Instantly perceiving it the wolves boldly tore at the tendon of the other leg and cut it in two. When the great animal sagged and fell on his left side, the wolves soon ended his life. Then after they had gorged themselves they went their various ways, one by one. Only the wolf that had been kicked remained behind; finally he got to his feet, limped to the carcass, smelled it and gave it a lick or two, but he was still too sick to eat and went away to the west.

Down from the far blue sky a turkey buzzard dropped on the carcass; then another and another came, until half a dozen of them were feeding on it. Ravens came, too, hoarsely croaking, and magpies and Clarke's crows fluttered and hopped round and scolded one another. To each of them I made my plea for help.

Suddenly they all took flight, and above their croaks and cries of distress I heard a loud rending of the air. Looking up, I saw a large eagle coming down with such tremendous speed that I thought he would be unable to check his flight. But check it he did and, with outstretched wings, came lightly to the ground some fifteen or twenty feet from the carcass. For a time he stood there, looking round in all directions; then he awkwardly waddled to the carcass and hopped upon it. Disdaining the meat the wolves had bared, he gashed the skin just behind the ribs and feasted on the liver, which he thus exposed. Finally, when he had gorged himself and flown away the smaller birds returned.

But they did not long have the feast to themselves; the shifting, eddying summer wind was carrying the news of the kill to all the beasts of the surrounding region. First some coyotes came and took their fill; then came a couple of alert kit foxes, and after them a badger that ate greedily and then burrowed under the carcass there to lodge as long as the meat should last. Later in the day the wolves returned singly, by twos and by threes; and among them came the old white leader with an old, grayish-white female that was undoubtedly his mate. He soon finished eating and then sat and patiently waited for her to take her fill. When she had finished the two trotted back the way they had come.

Late in the afternoon I heard rocks now and again roll and thud down the steep slope of the butte to the east of the cliff. At first I felt somewhat alarmed, for I thought that the Snake war party or some other enemies were there. Then I realized that a bear in search of mice and ants was making the commotion. Presently he appeared at the foot of the slope. He was a fine large grizzly still with faded patches of his winter coat upon him. Shuffling along the trail to the spring, he suddenly caught the odor of the carcass and, sitting straight up, eagerly sniffed the air. Then he began cautiously to approach it. At last his weak eyes saw it, and he leaped toward it, roaring loudly. He continued to roar until he had made the round of it and satisfied himself that he had frightened away any enemy that might have been there.

Then he made fierce onslaught upon the carcass.

He tore out huge mouthfuls of meat with so much force and haste that he actually shifted the position of the thousand pounds and more of meat and bone. He ate until he could not hold another mouthful and then walked round the carcass, seeking some way to cover it and make it his own. Here and there he tentatively pawed the ground and tore up a small clump or two of sage, but, finding nothing to serve his purpose, he abandoned the attempt and went to the spring to drink. When he was done drinking he plunged in and rolled over and over. For a time he lay flat on his back in huge enjoyment; and at last after he had given himself a good soaking he flopped over on his feet, came out of the spring, shook himself and walked slowly toward the west round the foot of the butte. I knew that he would go to the first thicket for a comfortable sleep, and that he would come again as soon as digestion had made room in his stomach for more food. Of course I prayed to him for help.

Now the sun set. First came a band of elks and

then some deer for their evening drink. They stopped short before they were within a hundred yards of the spring. Death was in the air: odor of blood, odor of wolves, strong repulsive odor of bear. The elks turned slowly round and went off to the east. The deer snorted and bounded back up the steep slope east of the cliff. After they had gone a young bull moose appeared, suddenly caught the dread odors, and, crouching low and stepping softly, sneaked off into the gathering night.

I climbed down from my couch, walked to the spring, and, though the water was still oily and odorous from the bear, drank and hurried back to my place. "O Sun! O Night Light! O Morning Star! O all ye Above People!" I murmured, "pity me. Help me this night to attain that which I seek!" It was a prayer that Red Eagle had taught me. Again I say that I must not be blamed for my superstition.

That night the moon rose late. I lay perfectly still under my warm robe and thought of the grim scenes I had witnessed that day. When at last the moon came up I saw that some wolves were again at the carcass of the buffalo. While watching them I fell asleep.

I awoke with a start and instantly realized that I had had a wonderful dream. Again I was out in the deep snow of a wintry plain. My horse had escaped from me, a blizzard was raging, and I was painfully forcing my way along the distant, timbered valley of the Two Medicine River. I was exhausted and freezing. I feared that I could never reach shelter. I cried out for help, and a distant muffled voice replied: "I will help you. Come this way. Follow me!"

I struggled on and, stumbling into a trail in the snow, followed it. I could not make out what kind of trail it was. I walked faster and faster and soon became warm and comfortable. Ahead I could see now and then through the falling snow the dim outline of the trail-maker; and finally I shouted, "You who are so good to me, who are you?"

"When in need always call on me, and I will help you!" came the muffled reply.

Then during a lull in the driving storm I caught

for an instant the shadowy outline of a buffalo bull sturdily breaking a way through the snow. I followed on and soon began to descend a steep slope. Then I knew that I was saved. There ahead of me, snug in the shelter of the timber that bordered the stream, was the camp I sought. Then my dream ended, and I awoke to find myself wet with perspiration.

Marveling at the clearness of my dream, I pondered it and gave thanks to the gods. I really believed that my spirit — my shadow — had gone forth from my body and had actually had that experience on the wintry plain. How was I, an ignorant youth, to know any better? For days, during which I was weak from fasting, my thoughts had been almost constantly on the ancient tale of the sacred bulls; and in whatever direction I looked from my resting place there were buffaloes scattered as far as the eye could reach. Seeing them constantly, witnessing the death of the lame bull and thinking about the ancient tale, I naturally dreamed of a buffalo.

Well, I was more than satisfied with the result of my fast. I waited impatiently for daylight, and with the first white light left my couch and started for home. The sun was not far up when I approached the great camp and met a rider out hunting the horses.

"Ha! It is you!" he said. "I heard that you were fasting at the cliff spring. You must be weak. Get up behind me, and I will take you to camp."

I was glad enough to comply, for I suddenly realized that my steps were becoming uncertain.

As we rode along my friend said to me, "Perhaps you are minded to tell me what kind of vision you had?"

"No, only my medicine man, Red Eagle, may know that," I answered.

"You are right, quite right," he agreed. "Few of us ever tell who our sacred helpers are. It is not safe; your enemy may use the knowledge to do you harm."

"What of the war party that I saw — Snakes — forty-three of them heading this way?"

"Ha! So you saw them! They drank at your spring, no doubt? Yes? Well, eighteen of them will never drink again. Night before last they rounded up a large number of our horses and drove them straight south into the gap in the mountains. They were heading for their West-Side country by way of Elk, or Yellowstone River, of course; but they got a late start with their plunder, and we soon discovered their trail. There in the gap we overtook them. They left the herd and even the horses they were riding and, like so many bighorns, ran among the rocks. We killed eighteen of them, my young friend, and not one of us so much as received a wound."

"I am glad of that," I said. "Twice they came to my spring. The second time they came from up on the mountain, and I knew they had seen our camp. When they started this way I nearly left my fasting place to run here to warn you. Truly I did make a start to do so and then because of old Red Eagle's rules for the sacred fast turned back."

"Right again!" exclaimed my friend. "The

faster may not leave his fasting place unless driven from it by the enemy."

We rode into camp and through it to White Wolf's lodge. I sprang quickly from the horse and entered, and what a warm, happy welcome I got from Pitamakan!

"Is all well with you?" his father asked.

"Are n't you hungry?" the women wanted to know and set about preparing soup and broiled boss ribs of buffalo.

Omitting my sacred dream, I told them my experiences at the spring while I ate sparingly. Then I went to old Red Eagle's lodge.

Greeting me kindly, he sent his women and children away and bade me relate my dream. He listened carefully while I talked, asking a question now and then, and when I had done he said: "My son, the gods have been good to you. He whom you saw in the storm was of course one of the ancient buffalo-men. You could not have a more powerful sacred helper. He has great favor with Sun. When you are in doubt, in need, sick, or in danger, you must always call upon him to help you and to intercede for you with Sun. Thus shall you be made happy; thus shall you survive the dangers of your life trail and reach great age. I am pleased with you and with what you have done. You can now go to war. You are no longer a boy, but a man; you are a defender of us, your people. There! You may go, my son. Go home to the rest that you need so much."

I went home and learned from the women that my almost-brother, ever thoughtful for me, was already riding to the spring for my bedding. I lay down and slept until long past noon and then went to the streamlet and had a good bath. I felt refreshed. But do not think that I was not grieving all through my fast at having disobeyed my uncle. It was the first time that I had done so, and what a price I was paying for it! Is-spai-u, instead of being safe in his stable in the fort, was perhaps lost forever. I sat silent there on my couch, staring at the little cooking fire, yet not seeing it. What chance was there of my ever regaining the horse! That was a vast country to the south of us, and many tribes of Indians peopled it. Which one of them had Is-spai-u — Crows, Cheyennes, Arapahoes, Sioux? Why, perhaps the thieves were from some West-Side tribe and had ridden straight south from our camp in order to throw the blame upon our plains enemies; perhaps even they were from some far southern tribe in the always-summer-land. It was well into April. Any day a steamboat with my uncle on board might arrive at the fort. Then he would send for me, and I would have to obey his summons.

I turned to Pitamakan. "Almost-brother, come with me in quest of Is-spai-u!" I cried.

"Yes; of course I will go with you!" he answered, as I knew he would.

"Not so fast, you young ones!" White Wolf said to us. "Our war party, which is on the trail of the enemy, will probably recover the black runner. Wait until they return — "

"I can't wait! Not a day! I must be off before my uncle returns to the fort and sends for me.

Without Is-spai-u I can never face him. You know what I have done. If you were in my place, would you feel like facing Far Thunder?"

"No, I can't say that I should. Not that I should fear him — "

"Oh, I do not fear him," I cried. "He would neither strike nor scold me. It would be his silence and the sad look in his eyes that I could not bear."

The chief nodded. "Still you must not set out at this time," he said. "Whether your uncle sends for you or not, you must wait until our war party reports. If they have Is-spai-u, good. If they have n't, then you will probably learn that the Crows did not take him; thus you will be saved a great deal of time that you would otherwise waste in the country of those enemies."

"Father is right. We must wait to hear from our trailers of the enemy," Pitamakan told me, and I said no more.

Days passed, miserable days for me. I had no heart for the hunt or for the dancing and visiting and feasting and story-telling round the evening lodge fires. Dreading to see one of our *voyageurs* coming with a message to me from my uncle, I kept watch upon the plain to the north. Ever in vain I looked to the south for the return of our war party.

On May 14th — the date seems to have burned itself into my memory — Antoine, one of our *voyageurs*, rode into camp with a message from my uncle to our chiefs. He had returned on the first steamboat of the season; the goods that he had brought with him filled the trade room and the storerooms.

With sinking heart I asked Antoine what my uncle's message to me was.

"Nothing," he replied.

"What, no word to me at all?"

"No. But this from Tsistsaki to you. She says that Far Thunder grieves because you did what he forbade you to do; that he grieves too over the loss of his fast buffalo horse. But you are not to fear; you are to come in, and she will do her best to make all smooth between you and him."

That my uncle had sent me no word of any

kind showed what he felt. He was himself so just, so straightforward in all things, that he could never overlook that one slip of mine. I was more than ever determined not to return to the fort; I would go in quest of Is-spai-u even if I went alone.

The chiefs held a short council over my uncle's message to them, and the camp crier rode through camp announcing their decision. The women were to have one day in which to dry the fresh skins that the hunters had brought in; then all would start early on the trail to the fort. I went early to bed to avoid talking with any one. I was too much depressed to talk.

But soon a commotion at the upper end of the camp roused me; people were running in that direction, and women were joyfully shouting out the names of husbands and of brothers. Pitamakan and I rushed out. Our war party had returned.

The sudden wailing of several women apprised us that there had been a fight, and that more than one of our warriors had fallen. It was some time before we succeeded in edging our way through the crowd and inducing the war chief's young pipe-bearer, No Runner, to come with us to our lodge. His widowed mother trailed along close behind us, calling out his name repeatedly in a kind of chant, and giving thanks to the gods that he had survived the dangers of the war trail.

White Wolf's women had rebuilt the fire, and with smiles and pleasant words they welcomed the young warrior and began preparing food for him. White Wolf himself came in, gave No Runner a hearty greeting and filled a pipe for him. I could not wait for the ceremonial opening of the talk — the lighting and passing of the pipe and then the chief's courteous invitation to the young man to tell us all that he and his party had experienced.

"No Runner, friend," I cried, "did you see Is-spai-u down there in the South Country?"

He gravely shook his head. "We did not, but we learned for certain that he was not taken by the Crows!"

My heart sank. I had made myself believe that the Crows had the horse, and that our party would at least see him in their herds. Where, I asked myself, should I find him?

White Wolf lighted the pipe and passed it to No Runner, who took a few whiffs from it, passed it back, and said:

"Take courage, Otahtoyi! We all now believe that Is-spai-u is not far away; we are quite sure that the Spotted Horses People have him. You remember that the heavy rain nearly washed out the trail of the raiders who took Is-spai-u. We found their trail plain enough up where Bear River turns from its eastern course and runs straight north to Big River. There the raiders left the valley and rode straight south across the plain. We soon found where six riders had turned off to the southeast — to get some meat, we thought. Then we saw where another and another had turned off in the same direction, and at last as we neared Elk River we had no longer a trail to follow. 'Ha! They try to deceive us, these Crows,' our leader said. 'They want us to go east, but we will keep on southward straight to their camp!'

"Southward we went and found two great camps of Crows in a long, timbered bottom of Elk River! During three days we watched the herds of those camps and saw not Is-spai-u among them. During three nights we searched for him in the camps, but he was not there. Then we knew that the raiders we had trailed and lost had not been Crows. So on the fourth night we raided those two camps, taking out their fast-running horses, and in the upper camp some of our men were discovered and four of them killed. What could we do? Nothing. We gathered at the appointed meeting place with the horses and waited and waited for the four to appear. They did not come; they were dead. We rounded up the horses we had taken, mounted and started home. Day and night we have ridden almost for five suns. And here we are with many fast enemy buffalo horses and very tired. Yes, Otahtoyi, friend, in the camp of the Spotted Horses People you will find your black runner!"

"But the Spotted Horses are not the only people

southeast of us. Beyond them are the Sioux; and a little more to the south, the Pani — " I could say no more; I was staggered at the immensity of the task before me.

"My son, take courage!" said White Wolf. "I firmly believe that Is-spai-u is in the camp of the Spotted Horses People."

"Almost-brother, we will start to-morrow night!" Pitamakan exclaimed.

"I must take courage! I do take courage!" I cried. "My heart rises. To-morrow night, brother, we start our great quest."

CHAPTER V

IN WHICH THE JOURNEY BEGINS

ON the following day while the people were preparing to move back to War-Trail Fort, old Red Eagle had his women prepare for Pitamakan and me a sweat lodge. It was made of willow twigs, which, having been stuck into the ground in a circle and bent inward, were lashed tip to tip to form a round hut about eight feet in diameter. The lodge was thickly covered with pieces of old lodge skin. When it was built we went in with the old sun priest, leaving our clothing and blankets outside. The women then passed in a few rocks that they had heated, and we rolled them into the little pit that had been dug in the center of the floor. Then the old man dipped a buffalo tail into a sacred red dish filled with water, sprinkled the rocks, and as the steam filled the little lodge began to pray earnestly to Sun and to all the other gods of the sky to preserve us from all the dangers of the long trail we were about to follow and to give us success in our search for the wonderful black horse. Between his prayers he sang some songs of his thunder medicine, in which we joined. Then we prayed each to his sacred helper — I to Ancient Buffalo-Man — to ask Sun to give us long and full life. And all the while during the hour or more that we were there perspiration dripped from our bodies. When the ceremony was ended we reached for our blankets, wrapped them round us, and hurried to the creek for a cold bath. We were deeply impressed with what we had done and confident that Sun would protect us. That afternoon after we had bathed I had a few last words with the *voyageur* who had brought my uncle's message to the chiefs.

"Tell my uncle," I charged him, "that I am sorry I disobeyed his order, and that I go now to do my best to recover Is-spai-u. Tell my almost-mother that, having endured a sacred fast and having had a wonderful vision, I now go without fear in quest of Is-spai-u."

The man stared at me, wide-eyed and open-mouthed. "Name of a name!" he exclaimed in his Canadian French. "I would not go down into that country of enemy savages, no, not for War-Trail Fort and all that is in it! Think of the risks! Change your plan, young sir, and come home with me to-morrow!"

"You have my message; don't forget to deliver it," I said and left him.

Toward evening Pitamakan and I got together the few things that we were to take with us — several pairs apiece of new moccasins, for parfleche soles wear out fast on the gritty soil of the plains; four rawhide lariats of good length; two small sacks containing needles, awls, sinew thread, matches in waterproof bladder skins, extra ammunition and large chunks of berry pemmican. Pitamakan decided to take along his bow and arrows as well as his good rifle. We debated whether to take our beautifully tanned and painted war suits and bonnets of eagle tail feathers and plumes. Warriors always carried them when going against the enemy, and if there were time donned them before a fight; but since we were going merely on a quiet search for Is-spai-u we decided to leave them at home.

The women gave us a last meal. We ate heartily of broiled boss ribs of buffalo and a stew of dried service berries. When we had finished night had come. We took up our weapons.

"We go!" Pitamakan exclaimed.

"Go!" repeated White Wolf huskily. "Go!"

The women bowed their heads. We knew that they were praying for us. We arose, stepped out into the darkness, and turned south past a hundred lodges where people were singing, dancing, and feasting. Far ahead of us in the gap in the mountains a lone wolf howled.

"I am glad to hear that; it is a good omen for us," said my almost-brother.

Up and up the pass we went along a trail that countless thousands of game animals had worn wide and hard; their sharp hoofs had cut deep into the bare granite. After three hours or more of steady climbing we were at the top of the pass. The moon had risen, and I saw Pitamakan shiver.

"Hereabouts lie the bodies of the Snakes that our warriors killed the other day," he whispered. "Here wander their shadows, perhaps to do us harm. Let us hurry!"

We plunged down the slope. The south side of the range was not heavily timbered; the going was good. When daylight came we were at the edge of a draw between two buttes in which was a trickle of water. Seven bighorn rams that were entering the draw stopped and looked back at us. I shot the leader and sent him rolling and bouncing down into the streamlet. We hurried after him and took all we wanted of the meat. Then we gathered some pieces of dry cottonwood bark, which burns without smoke, made a fire and broiled thick steaks and ate until we could hold no more. Then, keeping a side of ribs and the loin of the bighorn for future use, we moved on a half mile to an outstanding shelf of rock, where we intended to rest and sleep during the day.

The sun was now well up, but the air, which had not yet begun to quiver with the heat of the day, was astonishingly clear. Off to the west, the Belt Mountains, in which was the source of the Musselshell, though fifty miles away, seemed to be no more than a stone's throw from us. To the south, almost at the foot of the mountain on which we were perched, the valley of the river ran east and then bent northward round the point of the range and out of sight. It was sparsely timbered and had low slopes. Beyond it toward the Yellowstone were rolling plains with here and there a butte.

Valley and plain were alive with game. There were vast herds of buffaloes; some of them, formed in a waving line like a snake a mile or more long, were following their trails to the river. There were bands of antelopes — bright, quick-moving patches of yellow and white; they, too, were on their way to drink. There were elks and both kinds of deer.

As I looked at that vast stretch of plain and mountain with its thousands and thousands of game animals, I thought that, vast as it was, it was only a small part of the country of the Blackfeet and that with them I had my proportional share in it. All that great domain, extending from beyond the Saskatchewan south to the Yellowstone and from the Rocky Mountains east for something like four hundred miles, was mine as well as theirs; I had my share, too, of the millions of game and fur animals that it supported. I had not the slightest premonition that I was to live to see all that game exterminated, the country fenced by white settlers, and my people corralled in a reservation to starve and die! Oh, I was full of pride that morning long ago by the Musselshell, and so was Pitamakan. Twice we sang the Victory Song and twice the Wolf Song. Then after a short prayer we stretched out in the shade of a pine and slept long and sound.

We woke about four o'clock, refreshed, hungry, thirsty, and eager to face whatever was ahead of us, whether good or bad. Sitting up, we closely examined the mountain slope on either side of the great plain and the meandering valley below us.

All was peaceful; the game everywhere was quietly resting or grazing. Taking our war sacks and our meat and weapons, we went down to a streamlet, where we had a shower bath beneath a waterfall; then we ate another hearty meal of broiled bighorn meat. When night came we were at the foot of the mountains.

In the darkness we struck out across the plain to the valley of the Musselshell and followed its game trails until daybreak, when we found ourselves at the Big Bend, where the river turns sharply to the north and flows past the eastern slope of the Snowy Mountains on its way to the Missouri. It was there that our warriors had followed the trail of those who stole Is-spai-u southward on the plain. And there we were on the great war trail that was more used than any other in the country except the one that runs along the eastern foot of the Rocky Mountains.

There were heavy groves of cottonwood in the bend. With fast-beating hearts and eyes alert for the slightest movement in the thick brush that lined the game trails, we threaded our way through them. Because there were no deer, elks, or buffaloes in our way we were sure that a war party had recently passed that way and frightened them — a party that was probably hiding somewhere near us for the day.

At the edge of the river we drank all the water that we could hold, removed our leggings and moccasins and waded across.

As we hurriedly dressed Pitamakan whispered to me: "Almost-brother, no fire, no broiled meat for us this day!"

"No, nor rest for us here in the valley. It is too dangerous a place."

We sprang up from our dressing and looked round for a hiding place. High on the eastern slope of the valley and north of the bend was a thick growth of chokecherry brush, from which a deep, brush-lined coulee ran down to the river.

"Let us go there," Pitamakan signed to me, and thither we went, crawling on our hands and knees most of the way up the long, stone-strewn coulee, and pausing frequently to look backward to see whether some enemy had discovered us.

At last with bruised knees and smarting hands we crept out of the coulee into the leafy thicket, slowly turned round and sat up. Then we had our first good view of the valley below, and at once discovered a band of thirty or forty horses in a grassy park in the timber perhaps half a mile away.

"Oho, hai!" whispered Pitamakan. "What a narrow escape we have had! What if we had gone right into an enemy war party! The gods are surely with us, directing us even when we know it not; else why did we so cautiously sneak up into this brush patch?"

"As you say, they are with us," I answered, and added excitedly, "Look at that patch of brush on the ridge north of us. A man is sitting on the lower edge of it!"

Sure enough, there about three hundred yards from us was the enemies' lookout, lazily smoking a long pipe while he kept watch upon the country. He could not have seen us while we were crawling up the brush-rimmed coulee, but we could not understand why he had not discovered us when we crossed the river, or when we passed through the scattering timber to the mouth of the coulee. We finally decided that at that time he had been climbing up the ridge to his lookout.

When we first saw the man sitting there so near us, we were much excited but we soon calmed down and began to speculate how many there were in his party, who they were, and whither they were bound.

"The dog-faced enemy!" Pitamakan whispered. "How I should like to shoot at him with my good rifle! Far off though he is, I am sure I could kill him!"

"And have us killed! Once our enemies down there got after us with their horses we could not possibly survive."

"Of course! I was only saying what I should like to do," he answered.

"Well, I will tell you what I should like to do," I said. "I'd like to take two of those horses to carry us across the wide, waterless plain between here and Elk River. It is a long way, perhaps three nights' travel for us on foot — "

"But we can go straight south to the river," he interrupted. "That way is not far across the plain."

"And run right into the Crows. No; we must go more east than south."

"Even so it can't take three nights to walk to the river," he said.

"But it does! I know! I have seen a marking of this country that Big Knife Chief made long ago."

I referred to a map that Kenneth Mackenzie, then chief factor of the American Fur Company, had made in 1832, and that hung in our office at Fort Benton.

"Well, then, as you say, let us ride across that dry country. We will take, not two horses, but the whole band down there in the valley!"

"Haiya!" I cried. "If we could only do that! How angry the enemy would be, and how low-hearted! After making their long trail and risking their lives, to lose their rich takings! Oh, what a joke that would be on them!"

"But we can do it," he answered; "it's risky, but we can do it. They traveled at least all day yesterday and all last night, and they are tired. They will rest and sleep down there until evening, when they will call their lookout to go down and eat with them. At dusk they will start again on their homeward way. While they are roasting and eating their meat will be our chance! We can go down the coulee as we came up it — unseen. Then we can keep under shelter of the cutbank of the river until we are opposite the horses; thence we can creep out into the brush near them and wait for the right time to drive them off."

"Almost-brother," I answered, "it is a wild, crazy, risky undertaking that we are planning. Let us say no more about it now. Let us keep good watch and see what we can see."

The morning wore on; the heat there on the hillside became oppressive. Off to our right the

lookout, who had been half concealed in the edge
of the thicket, first hunched forward into the open
and then stood up to catch what little wind was
stirring. He was a heavily built man with a big
head. His hair stood up from his forehead in a
stiff roach, which made us feel certain that he was
an Assiniboine. The party, then, was northward
bound. We wondered whether they knew that our
people were right on their homeward trail?

Toward noon when the well-rested horses down
in the little park began to graze and move about,
we saw that only four of them, the leaders, were
picketed. When the loose animals formed in line
and headed into the timber on their way to the
river to drink, the four strained wildly against their
ropes and ran round and round, frantically nicker-
ing. At the sound the lookout stood up again and
intently watched the band until it had drunk and
come back to the park and scattered out to graze.
Then he lay down outside the thicket. But soon a
man, coming out from the timber three or four
hundred yards north of our coulee, called to him.

When he arose the Indian signed to him, "Do you see disturbance anywhere?"

"All is quiet," the lookout signed back after a swift glance round him.

"Come down and sleep," the other signed. "I will take your place."

The two met about halfway up the slope, talked for a few moments, and separated. We watched the Indian who was descending; he did not quarter off toward the horses, but went straight ahead into the timber whence his companion had appeared — proof enough that there, in an exceptionally heavy growth of tall willows under the cottonwoods, was the camp of the party. The spot was fully four hundred yards up the valley from the horses. Was there a guard with the horses? We doubted it. If there had been a guard, he would surely have taken the thirsty picketed animals along to drink when the band went to the river.

"Almost-brother, it begins to look as if we were to have that band of horses," Pitamakan whispered.

"It is but midday," I answered. "Later, when the sun is lower, we shall see what we shall see."

The new lookout was armed, not only with bow and arrows in a fur case on his back, but with a gun — a shiny, brass-bound "fuke." Like the other man, he was of heavy build and wore his hair in a roach. His leggings and shirt and even his breechcloth were apparently of common cow buffalo leather. We could have no further doubt; they were Assiniboines, our greatest enemy. Pitamakan kept a tense grip on his rifle and fingered lock and trigger. How his eyes blazed as he watched the ascending man, who was all unaware of our presence!

"Be wise! Be wise, almost-brother," I whispered. "You know you must not kill the man."

"The dog-face!" he hissed. "How I should like to count *coup* on him!"

The man, going to the edge of the thicket, stood there a long time looking up and down the valley and off over the great plain. Then he stretched himself comfortably on the ground below the brush. After our long night walk we should have felt tired and sleepy, but the danger of our position kept us wide-awake and alert.

"If we are to take those horses," Pitamakan said after the lookout had stood up, scanned the country, and lain down, "now while the enemy down there are asleep, is the time to start. Shall we go?"

Thinking of the terrible risk we should run, I did not answer him for several moments; but at last I faced him and forced myself to say, "We go!"

Straight through our patch of cherry brush cut the narrow, deep coulee. Noiselessly, Pitamakan slid into it, and I followed him. Then we began crawling down the rough bed. As I have said, it was deep and narrow, so narrow in fact that in places the rose-brush and sage that grew along the edges met overhead. All was well with us: we were creeping along noiselessly, without any trouble except the hurt to our knees, when suddenly, close ahead of Pitamakan, who was in the lead, a rattlesnake sounded its sickening whir. There it was, a big green-and-black fellow with a body as thick as my arm, coiled right in the center of the coulee.

We stopped and stared at it while it stuck its red-black tongue out at us and sounded its rattles again. Pitamakan flipped three pebbles at it, but it never moved. Here was a predicament; the snake might hold us there all day! We could not possibly leave the coulee and go round the snake without the lookout's seeing us.

I was becoming decidedly anxious over our situation when Pitamakan, after looking back, signed to me to turn round and go up the coulee. I did so, and he followed. On the edge of the bank above us was a thick clump of greasewood. He stood up and after peering through it at the lookout cut a stick of it and drew it down so slowly that the man could not have possibly noticed any movement. While he was lopping off the branches and the fragile tip I wondered what he intended to do with it. No more than six feet in length and slender, it was no weapon with which to kill a snake.

But now, "Ahk-a-kwon-i-man o-mak pik-sek-sin!" (Going to learn something, that snake!) my almost-brother whispered.

Untying one of his moccasin strings, he made a large noose, the end of which he fastened to the tip of the wand. Then I understood his plan. Back we crept down the coulee. Again the snake thrust out its quivering tongue and sounded its rattles. Slowly Pitamakan crept close and still more slowly extended his wand and lowered it. That was dangerous work. As I watched I held my breath. A sudden spring, a quick coil, another spring, and the snake could fasten its deadly fangs in Pitamakan's hand or face. Nine times out of ten that is the course a pestered, angry rattler will follow.

Lower and lower and so slowly that the movement was almost imperceptible, Pitamakan lowered the noose toward the snake's uplifted head. The snake never wavered, but continuously sounded its rattles. Down over the triangular, wicked head went the noose. Then with a quick yank Pitamakan drew it tight and with a mighty heave tossed both the writhing snake and the wand backward over my head. Thirty feet behind me the snake landed in the coulee and thrashed and flopped round among the stones. Pitamakan looked back and gave me a significant smile. We resumed our way down the coulee.

CHAPTER VI

IN WHICH PITAMAKAN RAISES
THE VICTORY SONG

THREE times before we reached the river we paused, slowly arose and peered through the brush at the lookout on the slope, and then, turning, looked down at the timber and the dense growth of willows in which we believed the war party was resting. All was quiet; so far the enemy was unaware of our presence. But our hearts beat fast when we arose to our feet at the mouth of the coulee and turned to follow the river.

True, we were in the shelter of a cutbank higher than our heads, and the soft sands made our steps noiseless; but we knew that at any moment some one resting perhaps at the edge of the high bank, or coming down to the river, might see us. As with cocked rifle and restless eyes I followed at Pitamakan's heels, I prayed earnestly to my sacred helper, Ancient Buffalo-Man, for help to keep me safe. We had gone not a hundred yards from the mouth of the coulee when we heard near the river an indistinct murmuring that a moment later we knew was the sound of men talking. Then how closely we hugged the cutbank, how breathlessly and slowly we sneaked along under it! My skin crept. Alternately I prayed to my sacred helper to ask Sun to guide us safe past this near danger and scolded myself for undertaking so mad an enterprise. A word from me, and we should never have ventured from our safe hiding place in the brush at the head of the coulee.

We passed by the talking men, and, though we expected every moment to be discovered, sneaked on and on. At last we reached a point that we thought should be opposite the horses. A few paces farther on we found where they had come down through a break in the bank to water. Taking their trail, we slowly and cautiously raised our heads above the level of the timbered bottom land. We feared that two or three of the enemy might be lying close to the edge of the park or sitting with their backs against a tree, but no one was visible.

"We have no time to waste," Pitamakan whispered. "Let us go on."

Getting down on our hands and knees, we crawled along the trail through the brush that fringed the river. Then we sat up. Still we saw no one.

"When we get into the open," said Pitamakan, "the lookout on the slope will see us. To make him think that we are two of his party out to water the horses we must appear as much like Assiniboines as we can. Right here beside this trail we leave our blanket coats and our war sacks. We will then enter the park from the side nearer the enemy, walk slowly out, and turn loose two of the four picketed horses. Then we will mount the other two and drive the band this way as if to water. Just as soon as we are in the shelter of these trees we will take up our things and head the band down the valley and out on the plain as fast as we can go."

"As you say; lead on," I told him, taking off my capote and laying it on top of my war sack and lariats.

Turning to our right, we went forward slowly at first, then more boldly. We kept in the thick timber and well back from the park until we were in line with it and the place where we had heard the men talking. At that point we turned again and side by side walked boldly out into the park. We were by no means sure even then that the horses were unguarded, but with every step we became more confident that they were. Once in the open we looked up at the watcher on the slope. He never moved. Of course some of the war party might at any moment come out into the park, but so far as the lookout was concerned we could safely go on with our work.

I believe that the most nerve-racking thing we ever did was to turn loose the two picketed horses, bridle and mount the other two and without unnatural haste drive the band into the timber. When I dismounted and took up the things that I had left beside the trail, my legs would hardly support me. I had to try three times before I could get back on my horse. There in the shelter of the thick timber Pitamakan headed the band; I turned them out of the water trail and down the valley. Lashing them with rope-ends, we urged them on until they broke into a trot.

Just as we had got them strung out in line and going well along a big-game trail, we heard wild yelling back in the park and saw three or four men coming after us as fast as they could run. We shouted at the horses, charged down on them, and with all our strength lashed their rumps with our rope-ends. They crowded one against another, threw up their heads, but refused to break into a lope.

"Push on through!" Pitamakan shouted to me. "Get after those lazy ones in the lead!"

As my animal was high-strung and eager to go, I found it easy to do as he said, and when I reached the leaders how I did flog them into a swift lope! The rest, urged on by Pitamakan, came thundering along behind me.

I heard a shot and, looking back, saw three of the enemy less than a hundred yards away. Neither bullet nor arrow had touched my almost-brother, and we were rapidly drawing out of range. I laughed and yelled; Pitamakan raised the Victory Song of our people. On we went through the long grove and across a wide, open bottom. We knew that we were safe from pursuit!

"Water!" I shouted. "We must have water before we go up on the plain." We turned the band down into the river, dismounted, and drank our fill and let the horses drink all they would.

"What a fine band of horses we have captured!" said Pitamakan as we remounted and drove the band back into the bottom. "Buffalo runners every one by their looks! Thirty-four fast buffalo horses! Almost-brother, let us head homeward with them."

"No!" I yelled. "Not for a hundred, not for five hundred, head of buffalo horses would I turn back! We started out to find Is-spai-u, and I must keep going until I find him!"

"Oh, well, as you say," he replied. "Perhaps we can cache the band somewhere out there on the plain and take them up on our way homeward."

From the tone of his voice I knew that he was keenly disappointed at my answer; but I could not face my uncle until I could give back Is-spai-u to him.

Out over the green plain we went at an easy trot, I in the lead while Pitamakan drove the band after me. As we rode I pictured to myself Mackenzie's map as it looked hanging on the wall of our office at Fort Benton, where I had studied it many times. A course east by south, I believed, would bring us to the Yellowstone River a little above the mouth of a southern tributary named Powder River on the map. I indistinctly remembered some of our *engagés'* saying that the Cheyennes frequently camped and hunted along it. I dropped back beside Pitamakan and asked, "Did you ever hear of a stream named Powder River?"

"Never!" he answered.

"Nor Bighorn River? Tongue River?"

"Ha! I know both of them!" he exclaimed. "One spring, when I was a little boy of maybe six winters, the Crows did us much wrong. 'We will teach those dog-faces something,' said Big Lake. 'They shall know our personality.'[1] He called our brother tribes to join us: the Kainah, the North Blackfeet, our allies the Gros Ventres, and even the Sarsi, who lived under our protection; and together we went south across Elk River right into the heart of the Crow country and remained there all summer. We camped all up and down Bighorn River and Tongue River, living upon Crow buffaloes and other game and catching many Crow beavers. The Crows — ha! — they fled before us, some to the south, some to the mountains. All summer long our war parties harassed them, taking many scalps and many of their fastest buffalo horses. Yes, truly we taught them how powerful we are. But they seem to have forgotten. Only the other day our chiefs were saying that we should

[1] An odd expression, exactly translated.

all get together and again drive them out of their country."

"Powder River, according to the marking of Big Knife Chief," I explained, "is the stream that runs north into Elk River, next east of Tongue River."

"Ha! You mean Plenty-of-Cherries Creek," he said. "Now, what right had that white chief to give the stream a name of his own? To all the people of the plains it is Plenty-of-Cherries Creek, and so it must ever be. We camped along it, too, in that long-ago summer. It is Crow country. We shall not find the Spotted Horses People there. To find them we must go east over a dividing ridge to Little-Big River. [The Little Missouri.] That's where we'll find them."

I took the lead again, and we rode steadily on through the waning afternoon and well into the night; we camped at the foot of a lone, flat-topped butte, where we slept until dawn. When we awoke, we were both hungry and thirsty. We had picketed four of the horses and hobbled several more, and the loose animals had stayed near them. Mounting two, we rode to the top of the butte to take a look at the country. A few miles to the east many buffaloes and antelopes were scattered on the plain, some of which were moving toward the ridge in long files, a sure sign that there was water somewhere along the length of it. Far to the southeast and east, perhaps forty miles away, we could see the dark breaks of the Yellowstone River. Pitamakan said that we should be camping beside it that night. We carefully examined our trail from the Musselshell and saw no signs of the Assiniboine war party. They probably had gone back south after more Crow horses.

A ride of an hour brought us to the foot of the long ridge and to a fine spring of water in a deep coulee. As we approached it, bands of buffaloes and antelopes ran madly away in all directions. We were far from the great war trail in a spot so isolated and devoid of timber that we doubted war parties or hunters ever visited it. We still had our lumps of pemmican, but we wished to save them for a possible time of great need; so, after we had drunk and had watered the horses, I went out from the coulee and shot a buck antelope, and Pitamakan gathered what firewood he could find, a few puny dry willows and stems of greasewood, which were not enough for our purpose. We ate the meat half raw.

While we were eating and resting I told Pitamakan that on Big Knife Chief's marking of this plain he had written, "No water."

"He guessed at that, or some one lied to him. Yet truly I did not know that there was a spring here; nor have I ever heard our people mention it. This is about the most unfrequented place in our whole country. Let us leave the Crow horses here. The grass is good, and there is plenty of water, unless they get homesick and strike out for the Crow camp, we shall probably find them here when we return."

"Yes, it is best that we leave them here," I agreed. "If we should take them to Elk River, they would soon be rounded up. I doubt not that many war parties pass up and down the valley, and of course the Crows often travel down it to trade at the big fort near the mouth."

We mounted the two horses that we liked most, spirited but gentle animals, and drove the others up round a bend in the coulee so that they would not see us leave and follow our trail; then we left the draw and struck off across the plain for the distant river. It was much farther than we had thought; night came, and still we seemed to be a long way from it. The day had been hot, and we suffered from thirst. We changed our course from east by south to due south and at midnight, as the Seven Persons marked the time, arrived at the rim of the valley, a mere depression in the plain not to be compared with the tremendously deep cut of the Missouri through the Bad Lands.

The moon, which had just come up, silvered the river. Along either shore stood a wide belt of cottonwoods and willows. Directly opposite us a small stream meandered through a wide, brushy bottom into the larger stream, and Pitamakan, pointing to it, exclaimed:

"Almost-brother, we have struck Elk River much higher than I thought we should. I know that little river across there; with our people I have camped along it. Rosebush River it is and no other."

"Ha! I had forgotten. I remember that upon Big Knife Chief's marking of the country it is Rosebud River."

"What matters the name! What I am thinking is that here we are too near the Crows. They may be camping near by. Look, no game is anywhere in sight. Tired as we and our horses are, we must go on downriver until dawn."

"But not until we have had water," I told him. "That we must have, and our horses, though we fight our way to it. I am choking with thirst."

Without another word he led the way down the slope, across a grassy flat, and into the timber. Though there should have been deer and elks in the bottom, not an animal fled before us. Near the river-bank we came upon a big game trail and got down from our horses to examine it; in the dust were many horse tracks, some pointing down and some up the valley; and mingled with them were the tracks of dogs — proof enough that they who had ridden along it were hunters.

"An enemy camp is somewhere near by," Pitamakan muttered. "I was sure of it when we were back there on the rim. Let us drink and return to the plain."

We went down a gravelly slope to the river. Our horses were extremely thirsty, but we dared not let them have all the water they wanted. We yanked them back from it, tied them to the brush, and drank ourselves, sparingly at first, then all that we could hold. Then we let the horses drink again.

I did not want to go on. "We should examine this near camp of hunters," I told Pitamakan. "They may be the very people we seek, the stealers of Is-spai-u."

"They are Crows and no other," he asserted.

"All up and down the south side of this Elk River is Crow country. The Spotted Horses People do not camp near it. I hear that they are no more friendly with the Crows than we are. We should only waste time looking for Is-spai-u here."

We mounted our horses, rode back to the plain, and, turning east, followed the rim of the valley, occasionally making a slight detour to the north in order to avoid a coulee. We had ridden only three or four miles when close in front of us some coyotes began yelping; a mighty chorus of dogs in the valley below almost immediately answered them.

"Ha! There is the enemy camp," said Pitama-kan, extending his arm.

We were rounding a coulee at the time, and upon returning to the rim we looked down across a wide bottom at several hundred new lodges gleaming white in the moonlight against the dark background of a big grove of cottonwoods. We brought our horses to a stand and stared down at the camp and at the many bands of horses grazing in the bottom.

"Our returned war party assured us that the Crows did not have Is-spai-u," I said, turning to Pitamakan, "but that is not proof enough for me. They were at two great camps of Crows straight south from the big bend of Bear River. This camp may have been here a long time; it is more than likely that our warriors never saw those bands of horses. We don't know who are in those lodges. They may be Crows or they may be Spotted Horses People. But no matter who they are I must make a search for Is-spai-u down there before we go any farther."

"I take back what I said there at the river," he answered. "It comes to me that we saw no lines of dragged travois and lodge poles in the trails either in the bottom or up here on the plain. If those are Crows they certainly were here or somewhere below when our men were at the big upriver camps. Yes, almost-brother, we have to look for Is-spai-u down there, but not in those loose, grazing herds.

If they have your black runner, he is picketed with the fast buffalo horses among the lodges."

"I am glad that we are of one mind. Let us plan quickly how to search the camp."

"There is only one way to do it," he exclaimed. "We will picket our horses right here and strike across the bottom to the upper end of the camp, go down through it, and thence back here. Let us hurry; dawn is not far off."

We tethered the animals to some stout sage-brush, and I was about to leave my war sack and my lariats there near my horse when Pitamakan cautioned me not to do so.

"They are of no great weight; keep them on you," he said. "We cannot be sure that we shall return here."

We went swiftly a part of the way across the wide bottom, and then more and more slowly as we neared the camp. Many horses were picketed between the lodges. How I hoped that Is-spai-u was one of them!

We struck the timber about a hundred yards

above the uppermost lodges. The dogs had become quiet, but now in answer to the challenge of a couple of wolves out in the bottom they again broke into a swelling, deafening chorus of howls and yelps. That was the time for us to enter the camp; once within its bounds they would probably pay no attention to us. Since they were all out in front of the lodges, we ran down through the timber, then turned and, walking out from it, began our search. As they ceased howling and came trooping back to lie down beside the lodges of their owners, a huge, wolflike dog walked sedately up to me, sniffed at the edge of my capote and with drooping head and not so much as a wag of his bushy tail turned away. Others that were watching him then paid us no further attention. So far as they were concerned we were safe from discovery.

If there is anything more trying to the nerves than prowling round an enemy camp at night, I should like to know what it is. Every step I made seemed to increase my fear. I not only had to turn this way and that toward every black horse that I saw, but I had also to look at the doorways of the lodges and at every dark object lying near them, for any patch of darkness might conceal a watcher wide-awake under his robe. There were numerous black horses, but no Is-spai-u.

Pitamakan pointed to a sun priest's lodge, banded with paintings of large red and black birds with outstretched wings. "I have heard of that; it is the eagle sacred lodge of the Crows," he signed to me.

When we had gone halfway through the camp another dog came to us and inquiringly sniffed at the skirt of Pitamakan's capote — just once — and then at mine; then, apparently convinced that we were of his people, he turned away. I had not the white-man odor, or there surely would have been trouble.

We moved on and on and at last approached the lower end of the camp and saw that there was no black horse among those tethered between the lodges or in front of them. Our quest had been fruitless. We turned to go straight out across the bottom but as we were passing the first lodge on our right the door curtain was suddenly thrust aside, and a woman who was starting to come out saw us plainly and dodged quickly back inside, wildly shrieking something to her man.

CHAPTER VII
IN WHICH WE BUILD A RAFT

WHEN the woman shrieked, Pitamakan need
not have called to me to run. Even before
he spoke we were both racing from the lodges
straight toward our horses. Behind us men were
shouting to one another as they sprang from their
couches to seize their weapons and rush outside;
women and children were shrieking; dogs were
barking. We had not gone the length of a bowshot
from the camp before several guns boomed, and a
ball thudded into the ground close at my right. At
the same moment a man came running toward us
from among the horses grazing in the bottom, then
another, and to the right and left of them still
others. Since they had been in the bottom guarding
their herds, it is strange that at least one of them
had not seen us approach the camp.

As we were now cut off from our horses, we
turned and ran along in front of the lodges toward

the nearest timber. Suddenly five or six men started from the farther end of the camp to head us off, and others, making a great uproar, came running toward us all along the line of lodges. Close upon Pitamakan's heels I ran as I never had run before. I had no doubt that my time had come.

Suddenly Pitamakan began shouting, "Come out, my men, and attack them!" At the same time he began to make signs as if to companions in the timber behind the lodges. Although the warriors who were converging upon us did not understand his words, they did understand his signs, and I saw them look back over their shoulders. At a call from some one they stopped and again looked back. Before they had decided to renew the pursuit we had got well past them. We had no more than fifty yards to go to reach the wood, and in spite of the arrows and the bullets that they sent after us we reached it safe.

There in the dark shelter of the timber we swung round with our guns at our shoulders, but our immediate pursuers had foreseen our action; not one of them was in sight; they had all dropped flat on the ground, where the scattered growth of sage and greasewood hid them from us. Along the line of lodges the other men had ceased running and were standing in groups, talking loudly. The men who had been guarding the horses were approaching them.

"We survive!" gasped Pitamakan. "The gods are good to us!"

"Yes; but let us go on," I managed to reply.

"No," Pitamakan protested; "not until we fire into that nearest gathering of men!"

"No! No! If we empty our guns, the whole crowd of them will come charging upon us," I objected.

"But we can run, too, and in the darkness of the timber we can surely make our escape."

"There is no strength left in my legs or breath in my body for more running," I pleaded. "Come, let us go! Even now those men out there are crawling toward us."

Though I would not admit it, the very thought

of shooting into that group of men, enemies though they were and keen for our scalps, sickened me.

"Oh, well, have your way about it," he agreed, and, turning, led the way into the depths of the grove. But several times he looked back at me and said, "I don't like it! I do not like it at all! We should have killed at least two of those dog-faces back there!"

As we recovered our breath we increased our pace, and after a swift walk of half a mile or more arrived at the lower end of the grove. Sheltered by the river-bank we slipped into the next grove, frequently looking to see whether they were trying to head us off, but no one was in sight. The Seven Persons had swung away round in the northern sky; dawn was near.

"All the men of the camp will be out after us at daybreak," said Pitamakan. "Let us raft ourselves across the river."

"Yes, if we can find the logs for it," I answered.

As the snow was melting in the mountains the river was in flood, and I feared that all the driftwood on the bars had been swept away; but within a hundred yards we came upon a great pile of logs, poles, and brush that the extreme high water of the previous spring had piled on a point. From the mass we soon managed to pry two large, dry cottonwood logs and pull them down the bank into the water. Then, taking off our clothes and wading into the water, we lashed the logs firmly together with lariats.

After laying a heap of brush on the logs and lashing all our belongings to it, we pushed our raft out into the stream. Then, with Pitamakan hanging to the front, and I to the rear, we tried as best we could to send it ahead. Though the river had meandered for a hundred miles through the warm plains, the water was so cold that we frequently had to crawl out and let our unwieldy craft drift as the current willed; indeed, all our efforts to guide it and quicken its pace had little effect. Dawn was upon us; the eastern sky was already paling. We feared that the enemy would discover us drifting there, but when we reached the farther end of the grove from which we had pushed our raft into the river the current carried us in under a high, curving cutbank on the north shore, thence across the river to the south shore, when ahead of us we saw short, choppy waves — sure sign of a stony bar and shallow water. Drifting into the rapids, we found the water no more than three feet deep.

"The gods continue to protect us!" Pitamakan exclaimed.

Hurriedly drawing the raft into shallower water, we first carried our things ashore and then, unlashing the logs, set them adrift and ran up into the timber to dress.

"This is no place for us to pass the day in," I told my almost-brother. "The enemy may cross in search of us. It is best that we hide well up on the valley slope."

"Yes, if we can find some brush up there in which to hide," he answered. "Let us hurry."

Taking up our war sacks and lariats, we seized our weapons and started out through the grove. Deer snorted at us, and elks trotted out of our way;

evidently the Crows had not recently been camping and hunting on their own side of the river.

"The dog-faces!" Pitamakan grumbled. "They
keep killing our game! We certainly must teach
them to stay in their own country!"

There were coulees running down into the river
bottom from the plain, and in the half light of the
early morning we went up the nearest of them. At
the edge of the plain it turned to the right into a
dense growth of sagebrush; so, having smoothed
the ground and made ourselves as comfortable as
possible, we opened our war sacks and ate sparingly of our lumps of pemmican while the dawn
revealed the valley and the plain to our anxious
eyes. We could not see the lodges of the enemy
against the timber on the edge of which they stood;
but we could plainly see the bands of horses being
driven in by their owners, who, of course, were
anxious to know how many animals they had lost.
Of course they had found our two horses picketed
on the edge of the plain, and we laughed to think
of the excitement the find must be creating among

them. What a buzz of conjecture and argument was going on there in the lodges about the number and the identity of the enemies who had raided them, why the two horses had been picketed on the plain, and what were the present whereabouts of the men who had left them there! Well, we did not need the horses; from now on we were better off without them, for, traveling on foot and at night, we were less likely to be discovered. We put away our pemmican; the little of it we had eaten had only sharpened our appetites, and Pitamakan called himself names for not having taken some of the dry meat we had passed in the enemy camp.

Soon after sunrise a large body of riders gathered in the bottom in front of the camp and turned down into the timber in which we had made our escape. In a short time, abreast in a wide line, they came out from the lower end of it and crossed the long, grassy bottom; then several of them followed the trail we had made in the willows fringing the river and entered the next grove. There presently they all gathered at the drift pile from which we had taken the logs for our raft. Our footprints and the marks made by the logs as we dragged them to water across the sandy shore showed them plainly enough that we had taken to the river.

They quirted their horses and, in hope of overtaking and shooting us upon our raft, rushed through the grove and out across the open point and into the next grove. We watched them appear and disappear among the groves as they rode down the valley until the maze of timber finally hid them for good. Sure then that we were safe for the day there in the sagebrush — we had been careful to leave no footprints in the coulee — we stretched ourselves on the ground and with our war sacks for pillows slept soundly, regardless of the heat.

The sun was near setting when we awoke hungrier and thirstier than ever. No horsemen were in sight. We wondered how far down the river they had gone in quest of us. In front of the camp the herds of Crow horses were still grazing, and many men were leading their fast buffalo runners into camp to tether them close to their lodges. That night, and no doubt for many a night to come, they would keep close watch of their horses.

When we were satisfied that none of our enemies were on the south side of the river, Pitamakan said: "Though we must eat, we must not use the rest of our pemmican. Let us go down into the timber; the deer and the elks are so plentiful there that I may get one with an arrow."

Pitamakan got his bow and arrows out of the case on his back, and we slowly went down the coulee. Then we followed a well-used game trail through patches of rose-brush and willows along the edge of the grove. The sun had set, and the game was all afoot. Some were feeding, others were going to the river to drink. One after another the wary whitetails winded us before we got within bowshot of them. Several elks gave us the merest glimpse of their yellowish-white rumps before they vanished into the brush. A lone coyote came into the trail ahead of us, lifted his sharp nose to the sky, and yelped.

"He laughs at us!" Pitamakan growled. "I'll show him who is the hunter!"

He threw a stick at him, and with a flip of his tail he too instantly vanished.

Night was fast darkening the valley; it would soon hide the game from us. We were thinking that we should be unable to make a kill when we saw five buck mule deer coming to water across the bottom from the breaks. Unlike the white-tails, mule deer did not lie in the cottonwood groves of the bottom lands during the day, but preferred the bushes where the coulees meet the plain. They were stupid animals that, when alarmed, gave a few stiff, high jumps and then stopped to stare at the intruder.

That they might not get wind of us we ran to get downwind below, crossed the trail they were following, and stood motionless against the trunk of a big cottonwood. Looking neither to right nor left, they came on slowly in single file. Pitamakan raised his bow and, when the leading buck was directly in front of us and no more than thirty yards

away, sent the arrow into his side clear to the feath-
ering. The buck gave a couple of awkward leaps
and fell. He was dead before his body struck the
ground, for the arrow had reached his heart.

Now that we had meat we needed a fire. We had
neither time nor light enough to build a war lodge
in which to hide the blaze from the eyes of chance
enemies, and we dared not make fire in the timber
where the flames would illuminate the foliage.

"Almost-brother," I suggested, "let us have the
fire in the bed of the coulee that we came down."

"Yes! Of course! There I am sure no enemies
can possibly see it unless they happen right on us,"
he answered.

We had hard work to gather before dark enough
dry fuel for our need and pitch it down into the
deep coulee. After we had the fire going well and
two sides of ribs, the loin, the tongue, and four big
steaks from the hams roasting before it, we went
one at a time to the river and drank. What a feast
we had, and how quickly it renewed our strength
and revived our spirits!

We had roasted ten times the amount of meat we could eat. Putting what was left to the last scrap into our war sacks, we resumed our journey down the valley. We traveled steadily all night and at dawn, after drinking our fill at the river, went up to the edge of the plain. There in a patch of prickly junipers we cut and cleared a resting place for the day. Before we slept we had a hearty meal of roast meat and took a good look at the country. Buffaloes and antelopes were now everywhere plentiful, and the river stretched eastward as far as we could see. We had come a long way from the camp of the Crows and took no more interest in their doings.

Pitamakan said that we could not be far from the mouth of Tongue River, where Elk River turned north to join Big River. It was best for us, he thought, to keep on due east from the mouth of Tongue River to Plenty-of-Cherries Creek, and thence go on across the divide to Little-Big River and the camp of the stealers of Is-spai-u.

"If they are there!" I said. "And, though we

find their camp, we may only learn that the Spotted Horses People did not take Is-spai-u!"

"Oh, cease that doubting talk!" Pitamakan replied in disgust. "I know that they have him! Take courage! Be cheerful-hearted! Think how wonderfully the gods have helped us and before you sleep call upon your sacred helper to ask them to continue to aid us!"

"Yes, I will do so," I meekly answered.

We awoke several times during the day, and in the late afternoon sat up hungry, thirsty, and eager to go on. The country seemed peaceful; the herds of game near and far were grazing and resting or lazily going to water as they always did when undisturbed by man. Nevertheless, there might be enemies down in the valley, lying like ourselves well hidden during the day, and we were taking no needless risk. We stayed where we were until night; then we stole down to the river, drank and bathed, ate some of our roast meat, and went our way.

Until the moon, now in its last quarter, appeared, we found traveling in the valley by night hard and nervous work. There was always the chance of our stumbling on a war party or on one of the huge grizzlies whose tracks were everywhere in the game trails and along the river shore. As every one knows who has read the journal of Lewis and Clark, they were fearless, savage beasts, were those game-killing grizzlies of the Upper Missouri and Yellowstone valleys.

Keeping well away from the timber, we followed now a hard-beaten game trail and now worked our slow way through wide stretches of giant sage-brush. It was a warm night, and snakes were abroad. Several times we heard the sickening whir of a rattler close either to right or left of us; once we heard it only a step or two from a trail that we were following. We made a wide detour round the point. At the lower end of a bottom we generally had to go over a high place that separated it from the next. Early in the night as we were going down the farther side of such a rise and could make out the dark blur of timber at the foot of it,

Pitamakan suddenly stopped short, reached back and warningly pressed my arm. "Listen!" he whispered.

I heard a crunching as of powerful bones between powerful jaws and a sucking and smacking; the sounds seemed to come from the timber not fifty steps away. We next heard a thud! thud! as of a heavy body slapping the ground, and then thunderous, hoarse growls of rage that echoed from rim to rim of the valley, and immediately afterwards a great crackling of brush. Well we knew what was taking place down there; two grizzlies were fighting over a kill of buffalo or elk. Without a word we turned and ran back up the point and out on the plain. When we paused for breath the bears were still filling the valley with the sounds of their mad rage.

"Give thanks to your sacred helper, Sun, and all the other Above Ones," Pitamakan exclaimed. "Again we survive! They brought that other sticky-mouth to intrude upon the killer's feast. Had he not come, the first one would have charged us and we should be lying back there mangled and prob-ably dead!"

"I do give thanks to them all," I replied. "Truly, we have had a wonderful escape. Now, almost-brother, let us abandon this dangerous valley and strike straight across the plain to Tongue River!"

"Yes, let us do that," he agreed. "The distance cannot be great, and anyway we were going to strike off east from the mouth of it. Yes! We go!"

To clear the coulees that cut into the plain we had to go still farther out before turning east. The bears had ceased fighting, and we wondered whether one or both of them were dead. Their bel-lowing growls had aroused all the other prowlers of the night. Up and down the valley and along the plain wolves were howling, coyotes yelping, foxes barking.

"Well they know what has happened!" ex-claimed Pitamakan. "They are all on their way to the feast that they are sure awaits them."

Out on the plain where the grass was short and there was almost no brush, we traveled much faster than we had done in the valley, and with a feeling of safety that we found exceedingly pleasant. We well knew that the dim, moving shapes that we frequently made out ahead of us were only buffaloes or antelopes that would flee at our approach. It was well past midnight when the moon came up. Its light, though dim, revealed to us immense herds of buffaloes and many bands of antelopes upon all sides of us. It was a land of plenty and quite as rich as ours, that land of the Crows.

As we went on the country became rough. Some time before dawn we came to the head of a coulee running east that Pitamakan said undoubtedly ran into Tongue River. Sure enough, a little farther on we came to the rim of the plain and looked down upon the stream, which wound through a narrow and sparsely timbered valley. We went down to the water and drank. Then we decided to go no farther that night, for we doubted whether we should find water again until we reached the next stream, which was Powder River, or, as Pitamakan named it, Plenty-of-Cherries Creek. Loitering on the river shore until dawn, we ate there our simple meal of cold roast meat and again drank all the water we could hold. In the dusk of early morning we crossed the river, went up the east slope of the valley, and lay down in a small patch of sage-brush.

The day passed without incident. We awoke several times and sat up and idly watched the buffaloes and the antelopes filing down into the valley to water and then back again to feed upon the rich curly grama grass of the plain. As Pitamakan remarked, the animals seemed as plentiful as the grass itself. At dusk we returned to the river, drank, bathed, ate more of our cooked meat, and then, climbing back up the slope, struck across the rough plain toward Powder River. Although we had not seen the Yellowstone, we believed we were only a short distance south of it. All through the night at our approach great herds of buffaloes fled with a rattle and thunder of hoofs. The pungent odor that rose from the sage and greasewood that they crushed was pleasant in our nostrils. Pitamakan several times hummed the little song that begins:

> Po-no-kah'-yo, ahk'-sa ki-ta-wat-op?
> Kak-si-mi'-yi ni-ta'-wat-op,

or in English:

> Elk, what do you eat?
> Sagebrush I eat.

We were so strongly determined to reach Powder River before dawn that we walked much faster than we had walked on any previous night, and on the downhill slopes we even broke into a trot. But dawn came, then day, and ahead we saw only the rough, rolling plain. Close at our right was a lone, slender butte. We climbed it and saw that we were still a long way from the river, fully ten miles, I thought. Thirty miles or more to the northeast we could see the dark breaks of the Yellowstone where Powder River joined it. I was intolerably thirsty.

"Pitamakan, almost-brother, let us keep on to the river," I proposed.

"No! The risk would be too great," he answered. "Just see off there the herds of buffaloes that we should frighten and so attract to us any enemies that may be hereabout!"

"But see how quiet the country is. I doubt that there are enemies within a day's walk from here! And we are so thirsty! Come! Let us hurry on across that stretch before the day grows hot!"

He shrugged his shoulders, a habit that he had got from our French *engagés*. "Oh, well, have your way about it!" he exclaimed and led the way down the steep side of the butte.

After traveling straight ahead for an hour or more, we had to begin turning out sometimes to the northeast, sometimes to the southeast, to avoid the herds of buffaloes and antelopes that were grazing or resting or lazily following deep-worn trails to the river. We had not gone halfway when Pitamakan suddenly halted.

"Something," he cried, putting his hand to his breast, "lies like a weight here within me! I am terribly oppressed! I have a sense of danger ahead! Almost-brother, my sacred helper is urging that we remain right here until night!"

"I have not that feeling at all," I told him. "My sacred helper tells me nothing. We have so far got round the game herds all right; we can continue to do so; and we are so thirsty we must have water soon!"

And indeed my throat and mouth were so parched that I could not talk plain; nor could Pitamakan. He shrugged his shoulders and without another word led on. A brisk wind had sprung up, and in order that the game herds should not scent us we were obliged to make longer detours round them. The country ahead was so rough that even from the ridges we passed over we could not see the breaks of the river; but by noon I felt sure that we could not be two miles from the stream. Wearily now we toiled up a long incline. To the north and the south and coming slowly behind us were many bands and large herds of game. For once none was in sight in front of us; but just as we were reaching the top of the slope the wind carried our scent to a band of buffaloes on the other side of the rise. We heard them before we saw them; even against the wind the rattle and pounding of their hoofs came plainly to our ears. They had probably been to water; and now, surging up over the crest of the rise at our left, they thundered off to the west down the slope. Almost at once all of the buffaloes within sight began to rush madly to meet them and join in their flight; the bands of antelopes, making for high points from which to try to see what had caused the alarm, looked as they ran like mere streaks of yellow and white.

"There!" Pitamakan groaned. "Trouble comes to us just as I knew it would!"

CHAPTER VIII

IN WHICH THE CHIEF ASKS MANY QUESTIONS

STAGGERING to the top of the rise, we saw the river close beneath us. In the narrow, partly timbered valley other herds of buffaloes and bands of antelopes had taken alarm.

"If my warning means anything," said Pita-makan in a hoarse whisper as he watched them, "it is that enemy eyes are on us right now!"

I did not reply. My eyes were greedily fixed on the river, sparkling between its green and shaded banks. "Water! I must have water!" I croaked and staggered down the slope. As there happened to be no game trail where we met the timber, we had to tear our way through the underbrush. Reaching the cutbank, which was four or five feet high, we dropped to the narrow strip of sandy shore, crossed it, dropped our rifles, and, throwing ourselves flat, plunged our faces into the cool water. How good it seemed! How refreshing! We took a few swallows, holding the water for a long time in our mouths, and then drew back, cautioning each other to drink sparingly. But how we had to fight the fierce craving that urged us to drink and drink until we could hold no more! We sat up and scrutinized the long stretch of river and the edge of the timber at our backs. There was not a living thing in sight.

"Almost-brother," I said, "not your sacred helper but your own self gave you warning of danger back there on the plain, and you were wrong. We shall be safe in the brush behind us."

"We shall know what we shall know!" he answered gloomily. Again we threw ourselves flat on the sand, and now drank more freely, though still not so deeply as we wanted to. Then as we sat up a deep, mocking laugh smote our ears! Whirling round to seize our rifles, we saw along the edge of the cutbank a war party every man of which had either a gun or an arrow leveled at us. One of them, a tall, well-built, fine-featured man, was signing to us with his hands:

"Back! Back! Touch not your guns!"

Pitamakan, sprawling out over the sand, was so intent on seizing his rifle that he did not see the signed command and probably would have paid no attention to it if he had. But, though frightened, I still had sense enough to realize that we could escape death only by obeying the order. Out of the tail of my eye I saw the men on the bank concentrating their aim on Pitamakan, ready to fire if he should raise his weapon. I made a spring and threw myself upon him.

With a wild yell he reached for his knife and turned to fight me.

"Don't move!" I cried. "Don't touch your rifle! If you do we die! So signed the enemy chief."

I released my hold on him and sat up. Lowering their weapons, our enemies seated themselves on the edge of the bank; that is, all of them except the leader. He sprang from the bank and with an amused grin came and squatted close in front of us and nonchalantly looked us over. It was hard to return his stare, but we did it, Pitamakan more successfully than I. In his eyes and in the determined set of his chin there were real hate and defiance.

Casting only an occasional glance at me, the chief stared superciliously at my almost-brother. After what seemed an endless time he laid his gun — a Hudson's Bay "fuke" — across his lap and, addressing Pitamakan, said in the sign language, "Now, the truth; tell me who you are!"

Pitamakan made no answer. A minute or two passed, and I could bear the silence no longer.

"Don't be so stubborn!" I hurriedly said to him. "We are powerless! Only by obeying this man can we possibly survive. Anger him and we die right here!"

Sullenly and to my great surprise he signed to the man, "We are Blue Paints" — that is, Nez Percés.

"Blue Paints!" the chief signed back with scornful emphasis and laughed long and loud. Up on the bank some of his followers tittered. "I have heard of the Blue Paints," the chief went on. "You — your people — live far from here on the other side of the great mountains."

"Yes."

"What do you here?"

"Nothing except to travel about and see the country and meet its people and make friends with them," Pitamakan answered, gesturing more freely and amiably now that he had become interested in keeping up the lie.

"We saw you coming from the west; the scattering buffaloes warned us of your approach," the chief went on. "No doubt you met the Crows back there and made friends with them?"

"They would not be friendly! We had a narrow escape with them!" Pitamakan answered emphatically, prefacing his signs with a mighty clap of his hands.

Again the chief laughed, and so did his men.

"And now you are traveling to make friends with tribes farther east — with the Spotted Horses People, perhaps?"

153

"Yes, with them, with whatever tribes we may meet," Pitamakan answered boldly.

For a moment or two the chief, leaning rigidly forward, stared intently into his eyes. Then he fiercely signed, "You lie! You are a Blackfoot!" And his men gave a thunderous shout of derision.

The sudden accusation almost stunned me, and if I did not turn pale with fear, it was because my sun-blackened cheeks could not change color. Breathlessly I watched Pitamakan to see how he would answer the charge. He appeared to be as calm as if we were with friends, and he smiled as he answered, "I a Blackfoot! No! I told you truly that I am a Blue Paint!"

"The Blue Paints do not wear Blackfoot moccasins. Look at yours! That embroidery pattern, those three diverging lines, what do they stand for but the Blackfeet, the Many Chiefs, the Pikuni — the three tribes of you!"

"Yes! They do mean just that! They are Blackfoot moccasins!" Pitamakan answered. "We visited the Blackfeet. They were good to us; their women gave us several pairs of moccasins; we were nearly barefoot when we arrived in that camp of friends."

The chief was plainly taken aback by the answer and was silent for some time. All the time I had been thinking that he and his men had heard me yelling to Pitamakan not to touch his gun, and that some of them had perhaps recognized the Blackfoot language — not the words, of course, but the sound of it. But no! Evidently none of them could say whether it was Blackfoot, Kootenay, Nez Percé, or some other language of the tribes to the west. That fear was gone, but still how terrible was our plight! How menacing was that long line of warriors on the bank, still darkly scowling at us! How ominous was the continued silence of their chief, who sat there all humped over, deciding what should be our fate! Sweat broke out on my face.

At last the chief suddenly straightened up and said in signs, "You say that you are a Blue Paint. I still doubt that you are, but I take your word for it. You look like a Blackfoot. You have had a narrow escape. We crept upon you as you were lying there drinking, and we were about to shoot you when I saw that one of you had yellow hair. I wanted to know what a whiteskin was doing in this country; so I ordered my men not to fire."

"We are glad that you did so; glad that we survive!" Pitamakan replied, and laughed happily, which was more than I could have done just then. He was a born actor.

"We are Spotted Horses People — "

"Is that so!" Pitamakan interrupted. "How glad we are to meet you this good day! Sun is good to us; he has led us through this unknown country straight to you, whom we are seeking with strong desire for your friendship. Chief, let us be friends!"

The chief paid no attention to his proposal. "You will take up your guns and come with us!" he ordered, and arose and turned down the shore. We got up and followed him, and his men, springing from the cutbank, fell into line behind us. After passing the end of the cutbank we entered the timber, went on for several hundred yards, and in the densest part of the grove came on a large band of horses, which four men were guarding. Screened as they were by the dense foliage, and a long way from where we had descended the slope, they could not possibly have been seen by us.

"They are all Cutthroat horses. Our taking!" the chief grimly said to us and with no little pride repeated, "Cutthroat horses!"

Then Pitamakan, omitting no opportunity to keep up his line of deception, exclaimed: "Cut-throats! We have heard of them. They are many and powerful, are they not?"

"Just nothing people! Cowards! We always outfight and kill many of them," the chief answered. Indeed, among the war sacks and the little piles of meat scattered round at the foot of trees we saw several fresh scalps stretched on willow hoops to dry.

The chief turned to his men, spoke a few words, and four of them left the grove to stand watch upon the slopes of the valley. He then signed to us: "We rode all night from well the other side of Big

River and up this river; we will rest here until sundown. Do you rest also. There is meat of mine; take what you want of it."

Here and there the men were building little cooking fires; so we made a fire ourselves a little way from the others and roasted and ate all that we wanted of the chief's buffalo meat. Then ostentatiously setting our rifles against a tree and laying our war sacks beside them, we went to the river and drank and had a good bath. Beneath the cutbank we talked about our narrow escape from sudden death and tried to guess what the future had in store for us. I maintained that all would be well with us; that, although the chief suspected that we were Blackfeet, we should have a certain amount of freedom in his camp, and that, if we saw Isspai-u there, we should doubtless find some way to recover him.

"As you desire things to be, so do you always say they will be!" Pitamakan exclaimed. "For myself, I know not what to think. Back there on the plain my sacred helper surely warned me of danger near, and so it was. We are in great danger now, I tell you. Remember one thing, almost-brother, that when I signed to the chief, 'Let us be friends,' he gave me no answer."

"Oh, take heart!" I told him. "I surely believe that all will be well with us."

We returned to the camp and sat by the smouldering remains of our fire. Some of our enemies were sleeping, some smoking and talking round their little fires. None approached us or apparently looked at us. We lay down with our rifles close at hand and were soon asleep. We were so thoroughly exhausted that we could not have kept awake.

Late in the afternoon we were suddenly aroused by some one's pressing us with his foot. It was the chief's servant, a young man of about our own age. We had noticed him cooking for the leader, carrying coals from the fire for his pipe, and making a soft grass couch for him. He handed Pitamakan a large cut of buffalo loin and said in signs, "You are to cook this meat and eat it, says my chief, for we shall soon be riding homeward."

The young man smiled as he told us that and altogether seemed so friendly that I ventured to ask him, "Where is the camp of your people?"

"Up this river."

"And how far?"

"Two nights' ride."

With that he looked over his shoulder at the men gathered round their fires and then covertly signed to us: "Be wise! Be very careful what you do! They over there are angry at you; they think that you lie to them! They plan to learn whether you are Blackfeet!"

As he hurried back to wait upon his chief Pitamakan turned to me and gloomily muttered: "You see how it is. We are in great danger. I knew it! My sacred helper continues to warn me of it! Here within my breast I feel a terrible weight."

"Well, anyhow, we have to eat," I said and proceeded to make a fire. But my cheerfulness was gone. I tried to think how our enemies could surprise the truth from us.

We roasted our meat and ate it half-heartedly

and then went to the river and drank. By that time the watchers had returned and eaten their meal, and the great herd of horses — more than two hundred — had been corralled within ropes that the Indians had strung in a circle from tree to tree. The chief pointed out to us the animals he wanted us to ride, and we lassoed and bridled them with our ropes, got our weapons and war sacks, and when all were ready, mounted and helped drive the herd out of the timber and up to the plain. The sun was setting as we topped the rim and headed due south to cut across a great bow of the river.

The chief had been careful to give us as scrubby a pair of horses as there was in the herd; but even so he took no risks with us. If we dropped to the rear of the herders, several of them always fell in behind us and stayed there until we were again abreast the line. Now for the first time we counted our enemies. There were forty-two of them. The chief and four others, his head warriors, keeping their mounts at a steady trot, rode in advance, and we drove the herd close upon their heels. Our animals were rough trotters and sharp-backed, and, although we used our capotes for seat pads, we were pretty well chafed before midnight. Some time after midnight the chief called a halt to rest and to change horses, and the two new animals we got were better than those we had been riding. Still, we were sore enough when we turned back at dawn into the valley of Powder River and entered a grove of cottonwoods that covered a long wide bottom.

We made camp close to the river, and the chief sent several men out to kill meat for the party. They soon returned with two horseloads of buffalo ribs, loins, and hams and two tongues for the chief. Pitamakan and I made our fire as far from the others as we dared, and so in a measure escaped the surly stares that most of the party gave us.

When the meal was done the chief sent four men to the rim of the plain to stand watch, and two to keep the horses close-herded in the heart of the grove. Then after several smokes every one made himself as comfortable as possible for the day.

To our astonishment the chief came and sat with us before our little fire.

"You had plenty of meat, ate until you were full?" he asked, and Pitamakan replied that we had eaten all we could and that we still had meat left.

"Now, you told me yesterday," he went on, "that you visited the Blackfeet. How long were you with them, and where did you leave them?"

"It was in the last falling-leaves moon that we found the Blackfeet," Pitamakan answered readily.

I thought that he far excelled the chief in the graceful, rapid use of the sign language, and I marveled too at the ease and naturalness of his lying.

"We found them on Big River," he went on, "where a stream that they call Bear River entered it from the south, and where stands a white man's house in which they trade. All winter we camped and hunted with our friends on both sides of Big River. Then in the new-grass moon we went with them to what they call the Moccasin Mountains, there hunted with them for a time and there left them and came on east and south to see this great country and try to make friends with those who live in it."

"In this new-grass moon, while you were with the Blackfeet, were they raided?"

"Yes. In the night by Crows. The Blackfeet lost two men and many horses — "

"Ho!" the chief cried in sudden excitement. Straightening up, he said in rapid signs, "Was one of the horses a swift black?"

"I don't remember," Pitamakan replied after some apparent thinking. "The Blackfeet have many swift horses, some of them black."

"And what did the Blackfeet then?"

"Many of their warriors went south, found the Crows on Elk River and took scalps and a large number of fast horses."

"Did they recover the swift black horse?"

"I have already told you I know nothing about a swift black horse!" Pitamakan emphatically replied.

"You are sure they were Crows who raided the camp you were in?"

"I was told so."

The chief took up a stick and idly smoothed the ashes of our dying fire, evidently considering what to say next. "That white trader you mentioned," he said at last, "his name is Far Thunder."

"How knew you that?" Pitamakan was surprised into signing.

"Why should n't I know? Our Earth Houses People friends [Mandans] tell us everything when we go to trade with them for their corn. We know that a great enemy of ours, a white named Sorrel Horse, lives with Far Thunder. Some day we will take his scalp! We know that Far Thunder has a Blackfoot woman named Little Bird and a relative, a light-haired young man named Red Fox!" And with that he sprang to his feet and after a sharp glance at me went to rejoin his men.

Pitamakan and I exchanged significant nods behind his back, and when he was out of hearing I exclaimed, "You saw the way he looked at me!"

"Yes, have n't I told you all along that we were in great danger, that my sacred helper keeps warning me of it? The chief surely believes that you are just who you are, Fox, and that I am your Blackfoot friend!"

"And he has never asked us to sit down and smoke with him!" I said.

Feeling too downhearted for further talk, we lay down side by side and slept fitfully. Late in the afternoon when our enemies began to move about, we again left our weapons in plain sight and went to the river to bathe and drink. We had no sooner taken off our clothing than several men entered the stream above and below us. Then the chief's servant came and bathed with us, signing that the water was warm and pleasant, and adding later that we should soon eat and then ride on up the river. When we began to dress he went into the brush with his clothing and beckoned us to join him.

"I told you," he said after he had looked up and down the stream to make sure that no one could see us, "that you were in danger. I say now that you are in great danger! I want to help you. I call upon Sun to destroy me if I be not all truth to you! Will you believe me? Will you let me try to help you?"

"Why do you want to help us?" Pitamakan asked.

"Because I like you. The first time I saw you drinking under the cutbank I liked you. Because I am not a Spotted Horses man; mine are the Wolf People [Pawnees]. I was captured long ago by this chief here, Short Spear. I am tired of being his slave. I want to help you escape from him, and I want to go with you wherever you go."

Pitamakan looked at me, and I at him. "He took the Sun oath just as we do," I said.

"Yes; I feel that he is to be trusted," he answered. Then he signed to the young man, "We take your word. We are glad to be friends with you. Tell us now what our danger is."

"You really are Blackfeet?" the other asked.

"Yes."

"And your friend here is the relative of the white trader, Far Thunder?"

"Yes," I answered.

"So believes the chief after he talked with you this morning. He believes that you two are looking for Far Thunder's wonderful black runner, which has been taken either by the Crows or by some people of his own who set out to raid the Blackfeet at the same time that he and his band started against the Cutthroats. When he told his men who you were some of them said it was best to kill you now, but he answered: 'No! I am going first to have some fun with them. When we get home I will give them a great surprise. Out of their own mouths and without a question from me they shall make known to us what they now so carefully conceal!'"

The young man suddenly dropped his hands with a warning look toward camp; three men were coming straight toward us on their way to the river. We had finished dressing; so we took up our capotes and started for the camp. When we passed the men two of them pretended that they did not see us and the third gave us a black scowl of hate.

We were much upset by what the chief's servant had told us. How was the chief going to surprise us into telling the truth about ourselves?

"We have been warned," I declared. "We simply will not show surprise, no matter what he does!"

Pitamakan gloomily shook his head. "That chief is wise," he said. "Unless we can have further talk with our friend and learn from him just how we are to be surprised, our end probably will come to-morrow when we reach the camp of the Spotted Horses People."

CHAPTER IX

IN WHICH WE REFUSE TO GIVE UP OUR GUNS

RETURNING to our place in the rest camp, we built a small cooking fire. Our new friend brought us meat and, with his back to our enemies, cautiously held up his right hand in front of his breast with the first and second fingers extended — the sign to be wise and wary. Then he turned abruptly and went back to his chief.

We broiled the meat and, having hurriedly eaten some of it, put the rest into our war sacks for possible use in an emergency, and we then helped to bring in the horses. The chief again gave us scrubs to ride. We all rode up out of the valley and headed due south as we had done the evening before. The chief and his favorite warriors, who were in the lead, rode so fast that we had hard work to keep the big herd close behind them. As soon as it was dark first Pitamakan and then I tried to get our friend to drop to the rear of the herders' line and explain how the chief intended to surprise us into revealing our identity. In turn we rode close beside him, not once, but several times, and even reached out and gave his leg a twitch, but, although we were sure he knew what we wanted, he paid not the slightest heed to us. Since it was impossible for any one to see us giving him the signal, we did not know what to think of his conduct.

"Do you believe he has decided to give us no more help?" I asked.

"I do not!" Pitamakan answered. "No one ever goes back on a Sun vow. We will cease bothering him. In his own way he is sure to help us."

"I give back to you your words, 'As you want things to be, so you say they will be,' " I told him, but with his rope-end he lashed into the herd and pretended not to hear me.

Again we halted at midnight to rest and change mounts, but our friend never came near us, and we dared not approach him. Then we rode on through the night, frequently frightening great herds of buffaloes that made the air tremble with

the pounding roar of their flight. In the morning
we saw far in the distance a range of blue mountains that Pitamakan told me were the Big Horns.
Then I remembered that I had seen a range so
named on Mackenzie's map. We were not far
from the river, and perhaps an hour after sunrise
we turned down to it. When we went into the
timber and built our little fires, the men opened
their parfleches and while they watched their
roasting meat laid out their war clothes and their
war bonnets. By that sign Pitamakan and I knew
they were preparing to make a triumphal entry
into their camp, which lay at no great distance up
the river.

Now was our last chance to learn from our young
friend how the chief planned to trick us. We hurriedly cooked our portions of meat, pretended
to eat, left our rifles leaning against a tree in plain
sight of our enemies, and, without one backward
glance at them, went slowly through the scattering timber to the river not fifty paces off. We
drank, moved back to the edge of the brush, and

stood there for what seemed an endless time, hoping that our friend would come to us and fearing that he could not leave his chief. We called upon our sacred helpers to take us safe through the fearful danger that faced us.

Just as we ended our prayers our friend came and, standing where he could look back through the brush at our enemies, hurriedly said in the sign language:

"In our camp is a very old Blackfoot woman who was captured when a little girl. She will be brought to the chief's lodge, will hear you talk to each other, and of course will cry out to you that you are her relatives. If I can go to her before the chief does and tell her that she must pretend not to understand your talk, all will be well. If I fail to give her warning, what will you do? I can see no way to save you."

With a hopeless gesture our friend lowered his hands. But, oh, how relieved I was, how suddenly confident that all would be well with us! When I saw the quick smile come upon Pitamakan's face I knew that his thoughts were the same as mine.

"Fear not for us!" He answered our friend so rapidly that his hands were almost a blur. "We both speak the language of the Gros Ventres!"

Then our friend smiled. "Good! Good! You survive!"

He hurried back to camp, and with light hearts we followed at a more leisurely pace. We suddenly became ravenously hungry. Roasting our meat thoroughly, we ate all of it while we watched our enemies painting themselves and getting into their war clothes. Never had we seen more beautiful embroidered and fringed shirts and leggings. Every one of the eagle-feather war bonnets had a long streamer of tail feathers that reached to the warrior's heels. Enemies though they were, we both admitted that in appearance they were the equals of our own warriors.

When all were dressed in their finery the chief gave the order to bring the horses, and soon we were all freshly mounted and back on the plain.

To avoid the coulees that ran into the valley, we rode straight for the junction of two gashes in the plain, in which, as Pitamakan explained to me, flowed the two main forks of the river. Now there was no game anywhere in sight, a circumstance that showed we were not far from the great camp; and presently we saw several riders come out upon the plain from the forks, stop and gaze and then go swiftly back. At the same moment the chief had us slow our horses to a walk in order to give the great camp time to prepare for our reception.

Pitamakan came sidling up to me. "It is a long time since we have used the language of our ally," he said; "let us talk it."

"I have n't forgotten how to speak it," I answered in Gros Ventre, and, as I believed, with almost perfect accent.

We could not have forgotten it. Gros Ventre children had been our playmates. After we had talked it for a time Pitamakan acknowledged that my pronunciation was perfect.

Now I had a thought as painful as a stab.

"Almost-brother," I cried, "the old Blackfoot woman may also know the Gros Ventre language. If she does, and if our friend gets no chance to warn her — to tell her who we are — then comes our end!"

The happy expression of Pitamakan's face turned to sudden grayness. "True!" he exclaimed. "Yes, just as sure as if she should hear our own tongue unwarned. And Blackfeet or Gros Ventres, to the Spotted Horses we are all one enemy."

"What can we do?" I asked. "How overcome this new danger?"

"We can hope that the woman does n't understand the language of the Gros Ventres," he replied. "That is all we can do!"

We soon came to the rim of the plain, and, looking down into the valley, saw the camp of our enemies, several hundred lodges set in a circle in a wide flat just below the forks of the river. Above and below it were hundreds of horses. A great crowd of people gathered at the edge of the camp gave a thunderous shout of joy and welcome when they saw us, and at a signal from Short Spear his warriors raised their Victory Song and brandished the scalps that they had taken. Down the slope we rode, driving swiftly before us the big herd of captured horses. The people rushed out across the flat to meet us, scattering the herd in all directions. Closely surrounding us, they called out to their loved ones and reached up eagerly to touch them. The men and the women and even the children had put on all their finery to welcome their braves, and, terribly anxious though I was, I could not help admiring the gorgeous color of the spectacle they presented and the wild enthusiasm that animated them.

At first the people paid not the slightest attention to Pitamakan and me, but as their excitement subsided and they began a general movement toward camp they began to point at us and regard us with unfriendly, suspicious eyes. When we were close to the camp Short Spear turned and signed to us that we were to follow him; and with four of his women and with several children running along at his side he led us to a fine, large new lodge and motioned us to dismount and turn our horses loose. When we had done that we followed him inside, and he gave us a buffalo-robe couch on the right of the fireplace and second from the doorway. The women and children came in, and the little ones, surrounding him where he sat at the back of the lodge, stared wide-eyed at us. The women, with never a glance in our direction, set about making a fire and preparing a meal. We noticed that the lodge had a high lining of beautifully painted cow leather, that it was furnished with many decorated parfleches for food and clothing, and that the couches were all of fine thick robes and had comfortable back rests.

The chief, after fondling a sturdy youngster in his lap and talking for a while with his women, suddenly turned to us and signed: "These children take and break everything that they can put their hands upon. Pass me your guns, so that I can be sure they don't break them!"

"No; we will keep our guns," Pitamakan answered.

The chief frowned, thought for a moment, and then emphatically signed, "I tell you to give me your guns!"

"No; we keep them!" Pitamakan emphatically signed, and, looking straight into his enemy's eyes, continued: "Chief, I give you straight talk. You shall know what I think. You do not intend to be friendly to us. You are minded to do us harm. We will keep our guns close beside us. If we are to die, others shall die with us!"

The chief's only reply was a grim smile. He spoke abruptly to one of his wives, and she took up her cow-leather robe and went out.

"He sends for the old woman," Pitamakan told me in Gros Ventre, speaking in a careless voice. "Take courage, almost-brother!"

"I have courage! I shall keep it!" I answered in the same light tone and laughed; but words cannot express the anxiety that my laugh concealed.

"We must not remain mute when the woman appears," he went on. "That would be useless;

sooner or later she must hear us talk; so it is best to let her hear us now and end it all one way or the other!"

"Yes, that is best," I answered. "And let me speak first. I shall say something that may save our lives, even if she does understand."

"As you say," he agreed. "Now let us put our thoughts upon our new friend; he may even now be warning the old woman about us."

"How can he warn her unless he gets her alone?" I exclaimed. "Small chance of that in this great camp!"

The women had set some meat to boil; we wondered whether they would pass some of it to us when mealtime came. We heard approaching footsteps and out of the corners of our eyes anxiously watched the doorway for the first glimpse of the woman who all unconsciously was perhaps to give the signal for our death. But it was the chief's wife that entered. She said something to him and resumed her place opposite us. Again the door curtain was thrust aside, and some men entered,

the four who had been Short Spear's leading warriors in the recent raid and one other, a man of
imposing appearance and of stern and haughty
bearing to whom Short Spear gave the seat of
honor at his right on his own couch. We thought
that probably he was the head chief of the
tribe.

The four had no more than taken their places
on the couch on our right when an old, gray-haired
man entered, followed by a slender, pleasant-faced
woman more than forty years of age. We gave one
quick, passing look at her and knew that she it was
that would decide our fate. Her features were different in every way from the broad heavy faces of
the women of our enemies and were typically
Blackfoot.

Short Spear motioned the old man to a seat at
his left. The woman seated herself just to the left
of the doorway, always the women's place. Then
once more the door curtain was thrust aside, and
in came our young Wolf friend and seated himself
on the couch between us and the doorway. We

exchanged quick glances with him, and he looked toward the doorway and slightly shook his head. He had not been able to tell the woman about us! I felt suddenly sick with disappointment. We had counted so much on his help! I cast a glance round the circle; though several of the men were talking in low tones, all of them were covertly watching us, and the four warriors were sitting tensely upright, ready to spring on us if we should try to use our rifles. While one of Short Spear's wives was talking with the Blackfoot woman, Pitamakan gave me an urgent look. Desperate and in deep despair, I said to him slowly and distinctly in Gros Ventre: "If this Blackfoot woman speaks to us, we die right here! She must not notice us in any way!"

I dared not look at her as I spoke, but even before Pitamakan answered me — I did not hear what he said — I knew that our ordeal was ended, for she was talking right along to her friend! What a wonderful feeling of relief swept over me! Joyously I cried out to Pitamakan,

"She does n't understand the talk of the Gros Ventres!"

"No!" he answered in a happy voice. "She never even looked at us when you spoke! Almost-brother, we survive!"

I glanced at our friend; there was a faint smile on his face. I glanced at our enemies; though doubt-less they were deeply chagrined at the result of Short Spear's test, they showed no sign of disap-pointment. I noticed that the four warriors next us had relaxed, and that the talk had become gen-eral. Short Spear handed a huge pipe to the man on his right to light and smoke first; and then he signed that we were to join in the smoke. As each man took the pipe and sent a few whiffs of smoke to the gods he offered a short prayer. So did Pita-makan and I, and if our hearers could have known what we said sudden death would surely have been our fate! We prayed that the Spotted Horses People might be destroyed and that we might suc-ceed in finding Is-spai-u. We were perfectly justi-fied in praying as we did, for had they not sent war parties to attack us at War-Trail Fort in a vain attempt to take the horse from us? Might they not have him now? Had they not killed some of our *engagés*?

"Yes; death to these men here and especially to this chief Short Spear!" Pitamakan said as he blew a whiff of smoke from his mouth and passed the pipe to the man on his right.

Outside we heard the soft treading of many retreating footsteps and realized that the people had stealthily gathered round the lodge in eager expectation of seeing us dragged outside to our death. I wondered why our captors had not killed us at once. I was soon to know.

Short Spear laid aside the smoked-out pipe. "We are glad," he signed to us, "that you are here with us this good day. Often have we heard of the Blue Paints, but, although the Snake People tell us that your people sometimes come over on this side of the great Back-Bone [Rocky Mountains] to hunt buffaloes, we have never met them. We should like to make a great peace with them.

Tell us, are they now hunting somewhere on this side of the mountains?"

"No; they are in their own country far on the other side of the Back-Bone, where the River of Snakes joins the Otherside Big River [the Columbia]. When they come over on this side they come in the moon of falling leaves and camp and hunt all winter long with their friends, the Black-feet."

"The Blackfeet!" the chief angrily signed. "Always the Blackfeet! Dog-faces! They are liars, nothing people! Not to be trusted! We are different: when we make friends with a people we are friends to them! You see what a rich country we have, with buffaloes, antelopes, elks, and deer as plentiful as the grass. Now, when you return to your Blue Paints will you tell them that we ask that they come and make friends with us and kill all of our game that they want?"

"Yes; I will give them your words," Pitamakan replied.

"That is good. I know we shall be good friends

together. Some Snakes who visited us last winter had among their horses a big, powerful swift horse of a color that we had never seen; all over its body it was speckled white and gray. They said that they had got it from the Blue Paints, who had great herds of that breed, the strongest and swiftest of all the different breeds of horses. I ask you, did they tell the truth?"

"Truth!" exclaimed Pitamakan. "Of all the different kinds of horses those white and grays are by far the best. They never get poor; they never tire. We love them much. We have hundreds and hundreds of them."

At that a satisfied grin overspread the face of the chief. He nodded to his friends, who almost without exception smiled and clapped their hands or rubbed them together in great contentment. Then all was plain to us; our enemies wanted some of the speckled horses for breeding and had spared our lives on the bare chance that we were really Blue Paints and would carry their offer of friendship to our people.

They asked us many more questions about our supposed people and country, all of which we easily answered, for several years ago we had passed through the country of the Blue Paints on our way to the mouth of the Columbia. Nevertheless, we were relieved when the women set food before us all, and our inquisitors, having eaten, went their various ways.

"Our relative appears to be contented and even happy with these people," Pitamakan said to me when the Blackfoot woman had followed her man from the lodge.

"And why not?" I answered. "Captured when young, she has grown to be one of these Spotted Horses People in every way."

"I doubt that," he said. "I shall talk with her."

Our Wolf friend, who had gone out with the guests, now returned. "I live in this lodge; this is my couch. I am glad that you are to stay here too."

"Yes; you three must be good friends," signed Short Spear.

"We need a bath; we will go to the river," Pitamakan signed.

"Yes, go, the three of you."

We lost no time in leaving the lodge. Above all things just then we wanted to talk with the young man.

Out at the edge of the great camp we paused and looked back with interest. The lodges were as large and as well built as those of the Blackfeet. There were few sacred lodges, but one of them especially interested us. Round its circumference it had two rows of huge red designs shaped something like a Maltese cross. Among the Blackfeet such a cross was the symbol of the butterfly, the silent flitting nomad of the summer that is the giver of good dreams. High on the back of every Blackfoot lodge the cross was painted in red and black — the perpetual prayer of the occupants for prophetic visions. I pointed to the lodge in front of us and asked our friend what the painting upon it meant. And when he replied, "Good dreams," I wondered whether at some time in the remote past the Blackfeet and the Cheyennes had been friends. Long afterward I learned that both tribes are of Algonquian stock, but I am inclined to think that their religious beliefs are not of Algonquian origin, but that the worship of the sun, which they both practice, originated in ages past in the wonderful semi-civilization of Central America, and that as it slowly spread northward the tribes of the plains adopted it.

At the river we found many bathers. So we went some distance upstream and then into the brush that our talk might be unobserved. There our Wolf friend wheeled round and faced us and, with an exclamatory smack of his hands, signed: "My friends, how I feared for you there in Short Spear's lodge! I got no chance to speak to the Blackfoot woman. But you noticed that when I followed her and sat on my couch I kept my gun close at my side. I tell you, my friends, if the woman had cried out when you began your Gros Ventre talk, I should have fought at your side until we were all three killed!"

"You are good to us — " I began, but he emphatically signed to me:

"Stop! That is nothing. I have big news for you. The horse you seek — the white trader's wonderful black buffalo runner — is here!"

CHAPTER X

IN WHICH PITAMAKAN RECOGNIZES
AN OLD ENEMY

ALTHOUGH we had strongly hoped that Is-spai-u was in the hands of our captors, our friend's assertion that he was actually in the same camp with us almost overpowered us.

"O Pitamakan!" I cried. "Did you understand? Is-spai-u is here! Here!"

"Yes! Yes!" he answered. "I understand! These dog-faces have him!"

"Tell us!" he signed to our friend. "Quickly tell us about the horse! Take us to him, so that we may be sure he is the one we seek!"

The young Wolf man laughed at our eagerness, then emphatically shook his head.

"No," he signed, "I will not take you to the horse, for that would arouse new suspicions of you. I tell you now that two of Short Spear's men still believe that you are just who you are. They say that the Blackfoot woman is cunning; that when she heard you begin to talk she concealed her surprise perfectly. They believe that with your first words you warned her not even to look up at you. So much I learned when I went outside and wandered here and there, listening to the talk of the men. They say that Short Spear is foolish to believe you when you say you are Blue Paints. They are going to watch you, and they will warn Short Spear to watch you too."

That was disconcerting news. Finally, I asked the young man to tell us what we ought to do.

"Not now! People are coming!" he warned us, and led the way out to the river, pausing to say something to several youths who came down the shore.

We bathed and put on our clothes, expecting to go back into the brush for further talk; but, giving us a secret sign of warning, our friend led us straight to camp and into Short Spear's lodge. The chief was asleep, and the women and children had gone out to leave him in quiet. Worried though we were, our long night ride and the excitement of our morning ordeal had so utterly worn us out that we and our friend too soon slept.

When we all three awoke late in the afternoon the women and children had returned to the lodge, and two visitors were smoking and talking with the chief, who filled a fresh pipe and signed to us that we were to smoke with him. The visitors passed the pipe along to us with such evident reluctance that we were almost certain they were the two who believed that Pitamakan was a Blackfoot and I Far Thunder's relative. I wondered if they had succeeded in reawakening the chief's suspicions of us. As soon as the pipe was smoked out, they left the lodge. They had paid not the least attention to us.

The chief toyed with his big, red stone pipe, rubbing its highly polished surface and admiring the rude yet lifelike carving of a bear that stood behind the bowl. Then, holding the pipe up in front of us, he signed that one of his friends, a Sioux, had given it to him.

"We are one with the Sioux," he went on. "We are many and powerful, and we are brave warriors; the Sioux are the same. Together we can destroy all the white men and all the plains people who are our enemies. We shall do that and have all the country and all the buffaloes for ourselves!"

Pitamakan pretended to be tremendously impressed.

"Yes, you are very powerful," he signed. "I shall tell my people what you intend to do to your enemies, and then I have no doubt that they will be glad to be friends with you."

Short Spear made no answer. He gave us a hasty, questioning look and then began to talk with his wives.

Food was soon set before us all — broiled boss ribs of buffalo, soup, and small portions of dried service berries — and Pitamakan and I ate a hearty meal. When we had finished and the women had taken up the dishes the chief filled and lighted his big pipe, smoked a few whiffs from it, and,

turning slowly, passed it to us, somewhat hesi-
tatingly, I thought.

"We are to have a big victory dance to-night,"
he signed to us. "You must see it; see our pretty
young women and our men, how graceful they are.
I will go with you when we finish smoking; before
the dancing begins I will show you our camp and
what a rich people we are."

It was near sunset when we started out with the
chief to see the camp, and our Wolf friend hurried
off to bring in the horses of the family and to
tether the most valuable animals close round the
lodge. He was late about it, and the chief spoke
crossly to him as he left us. We noticed that most
of the herders had finished their task; the camp
was full of horses on a short tether.

Women and girls were bringing on their backs
great loads of wood and putting it in the center of
the great circle of lodges. It was the fuel for the
fire that was to illumine the victory dance.

We skirted the open ground. As we passed
lodge after lodge the chief told us who owned them

and how many horses they had and how brave they were. He also kept calling our attention to the horses. Never had we seen so many pintos, all of large and powerful build and of various colors — black and white, sorrel and white, bay and white, and brown and white. Pitamakan was constantly calling my attention to the fine points of this horse or of that and declaring that, if we could only succeed in our present undertaking, he would later on own a band of them. The chief seemed to enjoy our enthusiasm over the pintos. I noticed that he watched our faces closely, and I wondered why. I thought I knew.

"Look out for yourself," I warned Pitamakan. "I think that this man intends to surprise us by showing us Is-spai-u."

He laughed. "Ha! We shall be glad to see him!" he answered.

The next moment we rounded a lodge and came face to face with the horse. Our hearts suddenly seemed to leap right up into our throats at sight of him. But neither by word nor look did we betray

196

ourselves. We could feel the chief's eyes boring into us and trying to read our thoughts. We gave the horse only a passing, careless glance, and Pitamakan, pointing to a near-by pinto, enthusiastically enumerated his good points.

We carelessly moved on somewhat in advance of the chief, but before we could round another lodge he tapped our shoulders and, pointing back to Is-spai-u, signed, "Don't you know that horse?"

We stared at the animal coolly, and Pitamakan answered: "No, we don't know him. Is he a swift runner?"

"Swiftest of all the horses of the plains!" the chief signed. "You should know him; I am sure you must have seen him a great many times. He is that white trader's — Far Thunder's — fast buffalo horse!"

"Ha!" Pitamakan exclaimed, clapping his hand to his mouth apparently in great astonishment. "It was a war party of your people that raided the Blackfeet at night when we were with them! I see now how it was; you sent out two war parties,

197

you and your men going against the Cutthroats, the other band going against the Blackfeet."

The chief's suspicion of us was now completely gone; we could read his thoughts in his face.

"It is strange that you don't know the horse after being with the Blackfeet all winter," he signed to us, and in his face was both disappointment and envy. "I should have him — " He looked cautiously round. "I, not the man of this lodge, should have gone against the Blackfeet."

Since the chief had no further object in showing us the camp, he led us to the dance, which had just begun. I saw at once that it was quite different from the victory dance of the Blackfeet. There were all of three hundred dancers dressed in their best. The bearers of the scalps that Short Spear and his war party had brought home had painted their faces black; the faces of the others were painted vermilion. The women formed one half of the great circle, the men the other half. Round the big fire they danced, and in a smaller circle within the great one a number of male singers and drummers danced round in the reverse direction. Now and then a warrior would break into the inner circle and shout out his *coups;* whereupon the great crowd of spectators would loudly applaud him.

"You see them all," the chief signed to us after we had watched the dance for a while, "their clothes, their faces, the way they dance. Are not the Blackfeet in every way far behind them?"

"Far, far behind!" Pitamakan answered. "How he hates the Blackfeet!" he said to me. "How he plans with Sioux help to destroy us! Little he knows how powerful we are, the three tribes of us and our Gros Ventre allies!"

We could not enjoy the dance, for the dancers made us feel that we were aliens; none of the young men took the slightest notice of us. We soon pleaded fatigue, and the chief told us to return to his lodge and rest. On entering it, we found that all the women and children were at the dance and the fire had gone out. We were rebuilding it when our Wolf friend came in.

"Put on just a little wood, so that the lodge will remain half dark," he signed to us. "Then we can be safe from watching eyes."

He drew in the door curtain and tucked the edges securely round the lodge poles. The fire — only a tongue or two of flame — blazed fitfully. Placing himself between it and us, he signed:

"The chief took you to see your fast buffalo horse, and you pretended that you did n't know him! Well, you have blinded the chief. He no longer believes that you are Blackfeet. As soon as you left the dance the two men who suspect you came to him, and he told them that they were crazy, that you did n't know the black horse, and that you certainly are Blue Paints."

"And they said?" I asked.

"They told him that he was the crazy one, and that he would soon find it out. They knew that you were Blackfeet, and they had warned Buffalo Back to look out for you. Oh, they had a big quarrel about you and finally parted in anger."

"Buffalo Back — who is he?" I asked.

"The man who has your horse," he answered. "And Buffalo Back told the two that they need not worry, that he keeps watch on the horse night and day."

"Friend, think hard now and tell us how we are to escape with the horse?" Pitamakan signed.

"I have been thinking about that," he answered, "but I see no way to do it just at present. It is best that you be patient. You must pretend that you are happy in this camp. You must visit here and there with me to get the people used to you. After a time Buffalo Back will not watch the horse so closely, and then we will plan some way to make off with him — and with other horses too. We must all three ride, you know."

At that our friend loosened the door curtain and stirred the fire, and we all lay down and went to sleep to the throbbing of the drums and the singing of the dancers out in the circle of the great camp.

The next day marked the beginning of a time of weary waiting and planning. Short Spear was now friendly. He furnished us with horses, and we went hunting with him; in the evenings we often were included in invitations to feasts and to smokes. Finally, he turned over completely to us and our Wolf friend the task of providing meat and skins for the lodge of his old father and for his four or five wives. But whenever we rode out from camp our two suspicious and watchful enemies went hunting too and kept always in sight of us. How we wearied of their constant espionage!

One evening we received an invitation to a feast in Buffalo Back's lodge and on entering found that we were his only guests. After his women had set large portions of pemmican in front of us, he started a pipe upon its round and asked us many questions about the Blue Paint people and about our wanderings from the far West-Side country. We answered all of them skillfully and convincingly. Then he told us about his raids on the different enemy tribes; north, south, east, and west — a long story — and boasted about the wonderful black horse he had taken in his recent raid on the

Blackfeet. He expressed astonishment that we had never heard of the animal and said he wondered how Far Thunder had come to allow such a valuable horse out of his sight.

That made me feel more bitter than ever against myself. In my mind I saw Tsistsaki, my almost-mother, going about her tasks sad-eyed and anxious, wondering where I was and praying for me, and I saw my uncle, oh, so grimly quiet at his work. No, I could never face him if I failed to recover Is-spai-u, tethered there within ten paces of me. But even now one of the women of the lodge was watching the animal while her man played host to us. In the daytime Buffalo Back slept out there and herded the horse on good feed close to camp. What chance had I to recover him?

The evening following our visit to Buffalo Back, Pitamakan, after long fidgeting on our couch and useless fussing with his gun and sorting the contents of his war sack, proposed that we go for a stroll through camp. Since I was tired I refused, and so did our friend, and Pitamakan started alone.

"I have again that feeling of oppression within me," he said as he arose. "My sacred helper is warning me of some new danger that threatens us."

I made no reply; danger was ever menacing us, I thought. I was so much depressed that I could not follow Short Spear's story of one of his raids, which he was signing to me. Presently he was invited out to a smoke, his women and their children went to gossip with their friends, and we two had the lodge to ourselves. Then Pitamakan returned, and the instant he came through the doorway I knew by the expression of his face that he had discovered some new dangers. He carefully replaced the door curtain and, turning to our Wolf friend, signed, "Are the Crows and these Spotted Horses People friends?"

"Yes, they are friends always," was the reply. "Did n't you know that?"

"No," he answered. Then he said to me and accompanied his words with signs so that our friend should know what he was saying: "You remember two summers ago when Far Thunder was building War-Trail Fort that we went up Bear River Valley one day? You were riding Is-spai-u, and a Crow war party tried to trap us? Do you remember that two of the men came out from the brush and signed us to advance and be friends with them?"

"Yes! Go on!" I cried.

"I was passing a lodge when a man was about to enter it. He pulled the curtain aside, and the light shone on his face; he was the Crow who signed to us!"

"At sundown a party of Crow visitors entered camp," our Wolf friend quickly signed. "I see now that I should have told you about it."

"We must go out from here right now!" I said, beginning to pack my war sack. "If that Crow sees us, we shall be instantly killed!"

Our friend tapped me on the shoulder, and I whirled round. "If you go now you go without your black horse. He is watched; you cannot take him. I see what we must do."

"Quick! What is it?" Pitamakan asked.

"This! The one thing to do!" he answered "The only time to seize the horse is at sundown after Buffalo Back has tethered him at his lodge and before any one begins to watch outside. We will go out now and remain in the brush a long time, then come back and sleep. At daylight we will tell Short Spear that we go to hunt, and we will never return to this lodge. Toward evening while two of us wait far out on the plain the other will go in, seize the black horse, and ride off to the two that wait. Then we will ride hard, hard, and escape from those who pursue us! I will be the one to come back and seize the black!"

"No! Not you! I!" Pitamakan and I both hastily signed.

"Let us go now into the brush and talk it over," he answered, and we hurried out and went down the river a little way.

The sky was clouded over, and there was no moon. The night was so intensely dark that we could not see one another's signs; so Pitamakan, making our friend lightly hold his hands, slowly and carefully signed to him, "Too dark now; to-morrow we will talk."

"Yes," the other answered in the same way.

Then Pitamakan and I discussed at great length our Wolf friend's proposal and decided that it was the one possible way to regain Is-spai-u.

We did not return to camp until we saw that most of the lodge fires had died out, and even then we approached our lodge cautiously. The heavy breathing of some of the sleeping women and children assured us that the Crow visitors were as yet unaware of our presence in the camp; so we went inside to our couches. Short Spear was still awake and spoke to our friend; the two talked for some time.

We left the lodge just at dawn; our friend, as he afterwards told us, had explained to Short Spear that we must make an early start so as to be the first to reach a certain band of bull elks that we had discovered far down the river. Eleven of the chief's buffalo runners were picketed round the lodge, and we took each his favorite from among them, saddled them with the saddles of elk-horn bows that Short Spear had furnished for our hunting trips, and were off before a single lodge fire was started in the big camp. Our one regret was that we were obliged to leave our war sacks; to have taken them, however, would certainly have brought a pack of warriors on our trail by sunrise. At the rim of the valley we paused for a moment and looked back; not even an early-rising woman could we see; and for once we had eluded the vigilance of the two men who were ever watching and trailing us.

We still had to complete our plan for getting away with Is-spai-u, and there was little time in which to do it. We halted a short distance out upon the plain and began to argue about it. Pitamakan and our friend both wanted to go back for the horse, but when I insisted that, since it was my fault that our enemies had taken him, it was my sole right to go, they finally yielded. We then decided upon our meeting place, a sharp butte

208

that stood twenty miles away on the rim of the river. As we talked we could see the peak of it, red with the first rays of the rising sun. We rode north and back into the valley; and then the two took my horse and went on while I made my way through the timber and the brush until close to the camp, where I hid for the day in a thick clump of willows.

Never again do I want to pass a day like that. The more I thought about the danger of my undertaking, the more fully I realized it. To seize Isspai-u there in broad daylight while people were moving round and Buffalo Back was close by in his lodge, and while one of his own women probably would be sitting outside on guard, seemed almost impossible. I was sick at the thought of the risk, and, oh, how I hated myself for having got into such a terrible predicament! Again and again I called upon Ancient Buffalo-Man for help! A thousand times I promised myself that if I ever got out of that trouble I would never again disobey my uncle!

But enough of my sufferings during the interminable hours of that long spring day. When evening came at last, I stole cautiously up through the timber to the edge of the great camp close to Buffalo Back's lodge. There was Is-spai-u tethered near it, and between him and me a woman was stretching a buffalo hide upon the ground to dry. I thought that she would never finish her task, but finally she pounded down the last peg and turned toward the lodge. A number of people were moving round a little farther on, but I decided that I should make my break the instant the door curtain fell into place behind her. Dusk had already come; in a few minutes Buffalo Back would order out one of his women to guard the horse.

Slipping my rifle under my belt, I stood ready. The woman went inside, and, with a fluttering heart and in terrible suspense, I walked casually out from the timber. I had perhaps fifty yards to go. It seemed to stretch into miles. I noticed that passing people were paying no attention to me and felt better. Then I kept shifting my eyes alternately from the doorway of Buffalo Back's lodge to the peg to which Is-spai-u's rope was fastened. I came to it and with trembling fingers freed the rope; then, coiling it, I moved on toward the horse and was almost beside him when one of the warrior's children came suddenly round the lodge, saw me, and shouted to his father.

Before I could mount the horse I had to bridle him; with merely the rope round his neck I knew that I could never guide or control him. Quicker than I have ever done it since, I loosened the noose and with a bight of it threw two half-hitches round his lower jaw; and then, just as I was springing upon him, Buffalo Back with mighty roarings burst out from the lodge and fired his old "fuke" at me and missed! Leaping swiftly, Is-spai-u carried me straight away from the camp; I had no need to use my heels in his flanks. A furious din arose behind me. Men rushed to mount their swift runners and bawled hoarsely to one another. Women shrilly urged them to hurry. Children cried; dogs howled.

I was halfway across the flat before the first of my pursuers left the camp; I was well over the rim of the plain before they reached the foot of the long upslope. When they came surging to the top they saw me far from them in the gathering night, heading straight west toward Tongue River. They followed, but they well knew that they could never overtake me. How long they kept on my trail I never learned. I rode three or four miles as fast as Is-spai-u could carry me; then when night came I halted and listened and could hear no sound of pursuit. At an easier pace I circled to the north, then east to the rim of the valley, and again northward along it; and about midnight I arrived at the butte, and Pitamakan and our faithful Wolf friend challenged me. For a few minutes what happy and excited talk we had! All through the night we pushed on northward, and at dawn we descended into the valley and hid for the day in the brush and counseled and slept until night came again.

We dared not take the direct route for home, for

we knew that our enemies would attempt to trail us that way. Consequently, we never knew what became of the band of Crow horses that we had hidden in the ridge where the long spring was. We followed Powder River down to its mouth, crossed the Yellowstone, went on to the Missouri and up it, and one fine day about ten o'clock in the morning rode through the great gate of War-Trail Fort. Our excited *engagés* and a host of Blackfeet immediately surrounded us. Then came my almost-mother and dragged me from my horse and kissed me and wept over me. And then came my uncle. I hung my head, knowing not what to say to him, but he merely put his arm over my shoulder and hugged me.

"There! There!" he said. "It is all right, my son! How glad I am to know that you are safe back with us again!"

And was n't I glad to be back, too!

THE END